Nurse Alissa vs. the Zombies V: Desperate Mission

Nurse Alissa vs. the Zombies V: Desperate Mission

Scott M. Baker

Also by Scott M. Baker

Novels
Nurse Alissa vs. the Zombies
Nurse Alissa vs. the Zombies: Escape
Nurse Alissa vs. the Zombies III: Firestorm
Nurse Alissa vs. the Zombies IV: Hunters
Shattered World I: Paris
Shattered World II: Russia
Shattered World III: China
Shattered World IV: Japan
Shattered World V: Hell
The Vampire Hunters
Vampyrnomicon
Dominion
Rotter World
Rotter Nation
Rotter Apocalypse
Yeitso

Novellas
Nazi Ghouls From Space
Twilight of the Living Dead
This Is Why We Can't Have Nice Things During the Zombie Apocalypse

Anthologies
Cruise of the Living Dead and other Stories
Incident on Ironstone Lane and Other Horror Stories

A Schattenseite Book

Nurse Alissa vs. the Zombies V: Desperate Mission
by Scott M. Baker.
Copyright © 2020. All Rights Reserved.
Print Edition
ISBN-13: 978-1-7351312-6-9

Cover Art © Christian Bentulan

To Alison

My wife, my soulmate, my best friend, and the love of my life. If not for writing, we never would have met.

Chapter One

3 March

This cabin will never be the same again – and I'm not talking just physically.

The deader attack yesterday tore this place apart. Both the front and kitchen doors were ripped out of their jambs by the horde. Chris and Steve remounted them last night, but it was a jury-rigged effort. The hinges are fragile. The doors don't open and close properly and are unable to withstand anything pushing on them. The windows in front were shot out by machine gun fire and the twin glass doors leading out to the deck were shattered by the deaders. Thankfully, Paul had stored pre-cut plywood in the shed to cover them. Chris and Steve are planning on a run to a hardware store in the next few days to pick up replacements for the ones that are broken. Even so, nothing will repair all the bullet holes, hundreds of them. Most are along the porch where Chris gunned down the deaders trying to get in. There are quite a few on the interior walls from the battle inside the cabin which will serve as a constant reminder of just how unsafe this world is.

Plus, there are hundreds of corpses inside and outside the cabin, all but two of them deaders. Chris and Steve dug two graves near the tree line for Diana and Brian and gave them a proper burial last night. They wanted to dig a third one for Nathan but I refused. Nathan will be gone soon enough. Digging his grave beforehand seems morbid. They're working now on removing and disposing of the deaders, and then will help Miriam and Rebecca clean and disinfect the place. Even so, none of us will ever erase the images of the carnage that took place here and the gory aftermath.

My room is a battle zone. Chris won't let me go in there until they're restored it to order, which I don't mind. I've been sitting in Nathan's room all night with him, a Colt in my lap, ready to put him out of his misery once he turns.

The cabin has lost all meaning to me. I used to view it as a safe haven, the place I had escaped to in order to avoid the nightmare enveloping the rest of the world. How fucking naïve. Now it's merely a location to hide in, a place to stay until we're killed or forced to run. Chris has been trying to reassure me that everything will be fine, that this was a fluke that will never be repeated. I'm not sure if he believes that. I don't. Our sanctuary was breached once and I'm stuck with the realization that it could, and probably will, happen again.

The violation of our sanctuary was also a violation of my sense of security. I no longer feel confident that we'll survive this apocalypse.

The worst part is sitting her waiting to mercy Nathan, my best friend and my lover, the man who saved my life on more than one occasion. I'm no stranger to death, even before this whole nightmare began. I've watched many patients succumb to their wounds in the ER. I even watched my mother die from cancer and my father of loneliness several months later. This is different. I never had an emotional bond with my patients and was helpless to do anything for my parents. Sure, I euthanized that old man in the hospital, left many others to their fate, and killed people when that gang attacked us. This is the first time I'll be taking the life of someone I care for. It hurts. The idea leaves me cold and dead inside.

I hate to say this, but I wish Nathan would hurry up and turn so I can end his suffering and get this over with.

"GRAB HIS ARMS," Chris ordered Steve.

The two men lifted the body off the kitchen floor, setting in flight scores of insects that scattered or flew away from the corpse. The stench hung in the air. One decaying deader was bad enough. Dozens made the odor unbearable. When combined with the congealed blood, bodily fluids, and internal organs covering the wooden floor, the air inside the cabin had become rancid. Chris doubted that they would ever be able to clean up the place.

They carried it through the living area and then outside to the side of the cabin where they piled it on top of the funeral pyre Chris had built last night. He found in the storage shed several pallets that Paul had used to bring in supplies, placed them on the ground, and doused them with kerosene. He and Steve then stacked the corpses on top of the pallets ten layers deep, each layer doused with more kerosene, and placed firewood between them. Chris would light it later tonight when the dark would conceal the smoke from anyone, or anything, nearby. He had picked the side of the compound to protect the cabin and hopefully keep the flames from being spotted along the road.

"That takes care of those inside and some from the porch." Steve paused to catch his breath. "What about those outside the cabin? There has to be hundreds of them."

"We'll worry about those later."

"Are you planning on burning them as well?"

"I doubt we have enough kerosene to take care of them all. The ones in the woods we'll leave for now. Those inside the compound we'll drag over here to get them away from the cabin." Bloated flies and wasps hovered over the dead, feeding off the remains. A few strayed toward Chris. He swatted them away. "Eventually we're going to have to find a pick-up truck and haul them away."

"A lot easier said than done."

"Yeah." Chris stared at the cabin where Alissa kept a death watch over Nathan. "But I'd rather do this than what she has to go through."

A GENTLE KNOCK sounded on the bedroom door. Alissa snapped awake, realizing she had dozed off. The notebook and pen fell out of her lap. She grabbed the Colt, ready to shoot Nathan. He lay in bed, still asleep.

The knock came again and Miriam realized it came from outside the room.

"Can I come in?"

"Sure."

Miriam entered holding a cup of coffee and a plate with a sandwich. "I thought you might want these. You skipped breakfast this morning."

"Thanks." Alissa did not feel like eating, but coffee sure sounded good.

Miriam placed them on the dresser. Alissa picked up the cup and took a long sip. "Thanks. I needed that. I started to doze off."

"You need to get your rest."

"I will when…." Alissa let her words trail off.

"How's Nathan doing?"

Alissa glanced over at the bed. Nathan slept restlessly. His hands and feet had been tied to the bed frame so he couldn't move. His breathing was steady though a bit labored. Half an hour ago, he had been tossing his head and mumbling, but had quieted down after a few minutes.

"He's not doing well. His wound is infected and he's running a fever of 102 degrees. I've given him antibiotics, but those will take a few days to work."

"I'm surprised he hasn't turned yet." Miriam regretted her words. "Sorry. I didn't mean to sound so callous."

"It's okay. I feel the same way." According to everything she had witnessed in Boston, those infected by the virus reanimated within seconds. By all accounts, Nathan should have turned right after being bitten by the deader. Instead, he lingered in this damnable limbo.

"Do you think he's immune?"

"No, unfortunately." Alissa remembered Dr. Edwards from Mass General on the first day of the outbreak. He had been bitten and didn't turn. However, Dr. Edwards showed no symptoms of infection and bled out rather than succumb to the virus. If Nathan was immune, he should be conscious.

"I wish there was something we could do for him."

"Maybe there is." Alissa felt a glimmer of hope well up inside of her. "Where's Steve?"

"Helping Chris remove the bodies from the cabin."

"Here." Alissa stood and handed Miriam the Colt. "Stay here and let me know if Nathan… if there's any change in his condition."

Alissa ran out of the bedroom and headed downstairs.

Chapter Two

ALISSA STEPPED ONTO the front porch, appalled by the cremation pile Chris and Steve had set up.

"Is everything okay?" asked Chris, expecting the worst.

"No change in Nathan, if that's what you mean." She switched her attention to Steve. "Is the ham radio working?"

"I checked it this morning. It was in the cupboard, so it's fine."

"Good. Please set it up. I need to contact someone." Alissa entered the cabin without further explanation.

Ten minutes later, Steve had the ham radio laid out on the gore-coated dining room table and sat in front of it. "Who are we contacting?"

"That group on the island off the coast of Maine. The ones you picked up the other day."

Chris moved closer. "I thought you didn't want them to know about us?"

"I didn't. But things changed in the last twenty-four hours."

Steve nodded his understanding and pressed the talk button on the microphone. "Calling 521st Troop Command. Do you copy? Over."

No response.

"Calling 521st Troop Command. Do you copy? Over."

The static stopped and a voice with a thick Maine accent came over the speaker. "This is the 521st Troop Command. I read you loud and clear. Over."

Alissa took the microphone. "This is Alissa. Who am I

speaking with? Over."

A pause. "Sparks."

"Sparks, do you have a doctor on your base I can talk to? Over."

"We have several. What do you need? Over."

"We have someone in our group who has been bitten by a deader. Over."

"I'm sorry, ma'am, but we can't help with that." Sparks sounded sympathetic to her plight. She knew she was talking with a decent guy. "Once bitten, he'll turn within minutes. Sorry. Over."

"He was bitten twenty-four hours ago and still hasn't turned. Over."

Sparks' tone became excited. "Hang on while I get a doctor. Please stay on the line. I'll be right back." He didn't even bother saying "over".

Eight minutes later, a second voice came across the speaker. "Alissa, are you still there?"

"I'm here. Over."

"Cut with the over crap. Let the military do that. I'm Dr. Carrington, the head physician here on Warren Island. Sparks said you have a person in your group who was bitten yesterday but has not turned. Is that true?"

"Yes. My friend Nathan."

"Can you describe his symptoms?"

Alissa contemplated lying about Nathan's condition, but knew that eventually the truth would come out. "A deader bit him on the knuckles. The bite wound is infected and he's running a fever. I've placed him on a regimen of antibiotics. So far his condition is stable."

"Was he fully bitten or just scratched?"

"He received deep bite wounds from the deader. Its teeth punctured skin and muscle. Can you help him?"

Alissa heard Sparks and Carrington talking in the background. Then the doctor came back online. "I don't know if we can. We've never had someone be bit who hasn't turned. But he might be able to help us."

"How can he help you?"

Carrington ignored Alissa's question. "Where are you located?"

"Near North Conway, New Hampshire."

"Hang on."

Alissa heard the rustling of papers in the background. After a few minutes, Sparks mumbled something about North Conway being there. Carrington came back online. "I have to go talk with my commanding officer. Are you in a location where I can call you back in about thirty minutes?"

"Yes, I am."

"Hang tight. I'll be right back."

The next twenty-three minutes passed interminably long. Alissa wanted to check on Nathan but passed on the idea. Miriam would tell her if he changed for the worse. Besides, she didn't want to miss the doctor's call back. Chris, Steve, and she were practically climbing the walls when Carrington's voice came over the speaker.

"My commanding officer gave me permission to bring your friend on the compound. According to Sparks, you're about a four-hour drive to us under ideal conditions. It'll take us the rest of the day to prepare a convoy. Give us your location and we can be there tomorrow afternoon."

Chris and Steve both shook their heads, not wanting the military to know where they were. Alissa ignored them. "That'll take too long. How about if we come to you?"

"You realize how dangerous it is out there?"

Alissa wanted to reply "no fuck" but kept her emotions in check. "I do, but we've already been through more than you can imagine. We'll leave in the morning."

"Have it your way. I'll notify the guards that you're coming. When you get to the gate, tell them you're here to see Dr. Carrington and they'll know to let you pass. Do you have a

GPS system?"

"I have a map."

"It'll have to do. You want to head for the town of Lincoln-ville on the coast. It's a few miles north of Rockport. We've built a fortified compound on the shore. You can't miss it." Sparks said something in the background. "What route will you be taking? We can send out a patrol to escort you in."

"Wait a moment." Alissa looked around for a map. Steve ducked into the kitchen and came back with it a few seconds later. The map had splotches of blood on it. She laid it out on the table and checked the route. "We'll take Routes 121, 126, and 17. That's a straight run to your base."

"That sounds good."

"Any idea what the deader situation is like between North Conway and Lincolnville?" asked Alissa.

"The area twenty miles out from the ferry is relatively free of deaders. We send out patrols every day to clear them. Beyond that, I have no clue. Sorry."

"That's okay. We have enough fire power to make it on our own."

"Great. We'll see you soon. Godspeed to you."

The other end of the radio went dead.

Alissa placed the microphone on top of the radio and turned to Chris. "Can I borrow the Humvee?"

"What for?"

"I need it to drive Nathan to Maine."

Chris smiled. "I'll drive you."

"No." Alissa shook her head vehemently. "This is not for the good of the group. This is personal. I'm not going to let you put your life in danger for this."

"You have no choice," said Steve, siding with Chris. "You can't take care of Nathan and drive at the same time."

"Sure, I can," Alissa argued. "I'll keep Nathan up front with me. Now give me the keys."

"No."

"Don't be an ass."

"I'm not. You know Steve and I are right. You can't do this alone. At least with me along, you stand a fifty-fifty chance." Chris moved a little closer to Alissa, his tone more serious. "Besides, this *is* for the group. You would do the same thing for any of us who had been bitten but not turned. You only think it's personal because it's Nathan. Am I right?"

Alissa hesitated before answering. "Yes."

"Then it's settled." Chris clapped his palms together. "We'll leave before dawn. Right now, Steve and I should get back to removing the bodies from the compound so the rest of you don't have as much to do."

Steve released an exaggerated groan and followed Chris outside. As they left, Alissa lowered her head. A feeling of disappointment washed over her. She had lied to Chris. He thought she would take this incredible risk for anyone in the group. Truth be known, Alissa doubted she would do this for anyone else other than Nathan.

Chapter Three

ALISSA SAT ON the edge of Nathan's bed. She placed her hand on his forehead. He felt warmer than before. Removing the infrared surface thermometer from the nightstand, she ran it across his skin. It registered 102.8 degrees. His temperature had risen since this morning. She dabbed away the sweat with a facecloth. Entering the bathroom, she took a second facecloth from the rack, soaked it in cold water, and wringed it out. Bringing it back into the bedroom, she laid it on his forehead and gently pressed it against his skin. Nathan moaned in his sleep.

Placing his hand on the mattress, Alissa carefully removed the bandages from his knuckles. The skin around the wound was bright red and pus oozed from some of the openings. The infection had stopped spreading and receded a bit, which she took as a good sign. She cleaned the wounds with alcohol, rubbed antibiotic ointment on the knuckles, and wrapped them in fresh gauze. Nathan winced a few times when she applied the alcohol and ointment, but never woke or stirred. Alissa grew concerned about whether he would even survive the trip to Maine.

Miriam opened the door and stuck her head inside. "Dinner is ready. Come down and eat with us."

"I'm not hungry."

"I know. But you need to keep your strength up. Besides, the group wants to talk to you."

"About what?" Alissa asked apprehensively.

"Nothing bad." Miriam opened the door wider and stepped aside. "Come on."

The two women headed downstairs. The others were already seated at the table, eating. Thankfully, Miriam had scrubbed down the surface and doused it in disinfectant. Shithead sat beside Chris, who occasionally dropped a tasty morsel off his plate which the dog eagerly devoured.

"How's Nathan?" asked Chris.

"Not good." She took the empty seat across from him. "His temperature has gotten worse."

"Is Uncle Nathan going to turn into a deader?" asked Little Stevie.

"I'm not sure." The thought of losing Nathan, especially to the deader virus, left an emptiness in her soul. "I'll know better once Chris and I get him to Maine."

"I wanted to talk to you about that," Rebecca jumped in. "I'm going with you tomorrow."

"Thanks, but that won't be necessary."

"It is and you know it. The two of you can't handle this by yourself. What if you have to abandon the Humvee and set off on foot? It'll take the two of you to carry Nathan. Someone has to be there to provide cover."

Alissa said nothing because she could not argue with Rebecca's logic.

"Then it's settled." Rebecca smiled, having won the argument. "The three of us leave at dawn."

Steve stared at his plate while cutting up a piece of chicken. "I still think this should be a four-person operation." He ignored the glare Miriam flashed in his direction.

"Are you volunteering?" asked Alissa.

"With this leg? The only thing I'd be good for is zombie bait."

Alissa grew confused. "Miriam can't go. She needs to stay behind and take care of you and the kids."

Kiera raised her hand. "He's referring to me."

"That's enough out of you, young lady," Miriam snapped.

"There's no way I'm taking you with us," added Alissa. "It's too dangerous."

"Come on," sighed Kiera. "I fought alongside you at the hospital and in the firestorm, saved your lives at the river, and, if not for me, Stevie, Connie, and Archer would be dead right now. I've more than proven myself."

Alissa looked to Chris for support. "Help me out here."

Chris hesitated. "She's right. She's one of the best fighters among us. Having Kiera and Rebecca along increase our chances of success."

"They also increase the chances someone will get killed." Alissa shoved her plate away. "I won't hear any more about it. What I'm doing is personal and I don't want anyone getting killed because of me."

"For you it may be personal," said Steve, his tone calm and soothing. "But we all owe our lives to Nathan. None of us would have gotten off Nahant if not for him, or probably even made it to this cabin. Let's be honest, we'd do this for any member of our group in the same situation." He focused his attention on Miriam, "Right, dear?"

Miriam's eyes tore into her husband for a few seconds, then her gaze softened. "Yes, we would."

"I can go?" Kiera barely contained her excitement.

Miriam inhaled deep. "If Aunt Alissa agrees."

All eyes fell on Alissa.

She shook her head. "I don't know."

"Do you want to save Nathan?" asked Chris.

"Of course."

"Then the more of us who go, the better our chances."

Alissa said nothing. Trepidation filled her. Deep down she knew they were right. Her original plan to drive Nathan to Maine by herself was asinine, a futile gesture of affection for the man she cared so much about that would almost certainly have ended in failure. With four of them going, they might succeed.

"You can go."

Kiera grinned, restraining her excitement so as not to be chastised by her mother again.

Miriam accepted the inevitable. "It's settled, then. After dinner, we'll pack four bugout bags and some medical supplies for Nathan." This time she directed her remarks to Alissa. "Finish your dinner. This will be the last decent meal you have for a while."

Chapter Four

ALISSA SPENT THE night sitting beside Nathan's bed, watching over and caring for him. This time, she brought Archer into the room, wanting to spend some time with him since she had no idea how long she would be gone. As Alissa should have predicted, Archer was in no mood to be affectionate. Each time he strolled past, she would pick him up and set him on her lap. The cat would allow himself a few seconds to be petted, his tail swishing in disgruntlement the whole time, then would dive off her lap and race to a corner where he would lick away the human scent.

"Asshat," she whispered with a chuckle after the fifth failed attempt.

Alissa moved her wing-backed chair closer to the bed. She leaned against the cushioned back, rested her legs on the bed near Nathan, and closed her eyes. With her left hand, she reached out and wrapped her fingers around Nathan's bound palm. For a moment, she thought his fingers closed ever so slightly around hers. She opened her eyes. They had not. Other than an occasional fitful stir, he had not moved in hours. Alissa dismissed it as wishful thinking.

No, she corrected herself. *It's a positive sign that he'll be fine.*

Alissa started to doze off when something heavy landed on her chest. She jumped, her mind warning her it might be a deader. Archer stared up at her. He walked up her chest, purring loudly, and rubbed his forehead against Alissa's. She returned the gesture. After a few seconds of affection, Archer made his way to her lap and curled up. Alissa reached down and petted him, eliciting more purrs. Archer raised his head long enough to lick her fingers a few times and then settled down for a nap.

Alissa did the same, finding solace in holding the two beings she cared for most in this world.

KIERA FINISHED GETTING ready for tomorrow then headed downstairs to find her mother. Miriam was on her hands and knees, a bucket of brackish water in front of her, using a soiled towel to wipe the gore off the floor. Little Stevie did the same to the walls while Connie worked on the furniture. When Miriam reached a spot of congealed blood that had dried, she removed a brush from the bucket and scrubbed the floor clean.

"Can I help?"

"Thanks, but you need to rest for tomorrow."

"I'm too pumped up to rest."

"If you insist." Miriam sat up on her knees and pointed to the kitchen. "There's an extra bucket and some towels drying out in the sink."

Kiera made her way across the living area. Her mother had already cleaned the kitchen. Kiera smiled. Typical. Her mother always had been a neat freak, unlike herself. She took the empty bucket off the counter, poured in some dish washing liquid, and placed it under the faucet. As the bucket filled with water, Kiera examined the drying towels. They all had been stained with blood.

When the bucket was full, she took it and the towels into the living room, got down on her hands and knees by her mother, and started to clean. Neither women spoke, each enjoying the company of the other, both knowing full well they might never see each other after tomorrow.

ALL THE PREPARATIONS for the journey to Maine had been made prior to everyone turning in for the night, though no one slept well.

They all gathered around the Humvee as the first shades of orange lit up the sky to the east. Alissa and Chris carried Nathan from the bedroom and laid him in back of the Humvee, stretching him out in the rear cargo bay with his feet near the hatch and his head resting between Alissa and Rebecca in the back seat. She tied Nathan's feet and hands together and wrapped gauze around his mouth so, if he turned, he could not bite anybody. Shithead curled up in the rear bed at his feet, resting among the bug out bags, anxious for the upcoming adventure.

Chris had attached the .50 caliber machine gun on the Humvee's hatch mount and loaded a full case of ammunition into the feed tray in case they needed it. He would drive and Kiera would navigate from the passenger's seat. She stood outside the vehicle talking with her family. All of them going on this journey wore their leather pants and jackets.

Miriam hugged Kiera, holding her much longer than her daughter wanted judging by the look of discomfort on her face. Miriam eventually broke the embrace but still held Kiera's hands. "Take care of yourself and don't do anything danger-ous."

Steve huffed. "For God's sake. She's driving to a military base in Maine through deader country. What can be more dangerous than that?"

"Don't remind me."

"I'll be fine," Kiera assured her mother, failing to curb her annoyance. "I'll be with Chris."

"And Alissa and Rebecca," Chris corrected from behind the steering wheel.

Little Stevie stepped up to his sister. "Hold out your hands and close your eyes." He placed something in her hands. "You can open them."

Kiera stared at a five-inch, plastic figurine of Spiderman. "Stevie, I can't take this. It's your good luck charm."

"You need the luck more than me. Besides, you have to stay safe and bring it back to me."

"Thank you." Kiera sniffed back a tear and held Little Stevie close. Now it was her brother's turn to be uncomfortable with affection. Kiera unbuttoned her left shirt pocket and slid Spiderman inside so his upper body showed and his arms rested on the outside of her shirt. She patted him for good luck.

Steve stepped forward. "Kick ass and take names."

"And when I come back, I'll kick the asses of those whose name I took."

"That's my girl." Steve hugged Kiera, holding it for several seconds. "I love you and I'm proud of you."

When Steve let go, Kiera headed for the Humvee. Miriam jumped in front of Kiera and hugged her daughter again. "I love you so much."

"Mom." This time Kiera's tone lacked its usual annoyance. She hugged her mother in return. "I love you, too."

Kiera climbed into the passenger seat and whispered to Chris, "Let's get out of here while we can."

As Chris pulled away, those staying behind stood in the center of the driveway and waved. Little Stevie and Connie each wrapped an arm around Miriam. The Humvee passed through the pushed aside gates, another reminder of the nightmare they recently endured.

The reminders continued as they headed south along Route 302 to North Conway and through the destroyed town. Nothing remained except the burnt-out hulks of buildings and the occasional charred deader. Staying on Route 302, they made their way through the decimated forest where the inferno of a few weeks ago had begun. Several minutes later, they exited the devastated area and entered a forest-enshrouded road untouched by the conflagration. A sign up ahead welcomed them to Maine.

It was not lost on any of them that they were entering territory they had never explored before.

Chapter Five

THEY DROVE FOR an hour, passing through a few small, deserted towns. Other than some wildlife that had slowly started to take over the area, there were no indications of looting or violence and, thank God, no deaders.

Alissa felt Nathan's forehead. He still ran a fever, but it did not seem as bad as before. After wiping his brow with a facecloth, she took his temperature with the infrared surface thermometer. It read 101.9 degrees.

"Where are we?" she asked.

Kiera checked the map. "The town up ahead is Naples. We're about three hours away from the coast."

"It's strange we've seen no one around," said Rebecca. "Everyone must have left before the deaders got this far."

"Not everyone," corrected Chris. "We're being watched."

"Where?"

"Up ahead in that farmhouse."

The three women focused their attention on a farm ahead of them on the left side of the road. A red barn stood near the woods and a white, three-story house sat thirty yards from the road. A curtain on one of the side windows on the first floor was pulled aside. An elderly man's face stared out at them. As the Humvee drew closer, the man let the curtain fall back into place. When they passed the house, he watched them from the front windows, a shotgun visible in his hands.

"He's scared," said Rebecca.

"He's cautious." Chris kept on driving. "Do you blame

him?"

"Sadly, no."

Chris checked his side mirror as they drove away. The man watched them from one of the side windows. Chris focused his attention back onto the road, though his thoughts went back to the old man. Since teaming up with Alissa's group, he had forgotten what it had been like to be on your own during a deader outbreak, the uncertainty, the fear, the loneliness. Granted, he had seen more action in his brief time with the group than he had before, but now he had friends. They looked out for each other in combat and enjoyed each other's company. Chris would never go back to being a loner. Part of him wondered what the poor guy must have endured on his own for so long.

Just before they rounded a bend in the road, Chris checked his side mirror one more time. The old man kept a close eye on them.

AFTER A FEW miles, Chris came to a stop.

"Is anything wrong?" asked Alissa nervously.

"There's a tree blocking the road."

"Can we go around it?" Rebecca suggested.

"No. It's across the road and shoulders. It's not a problem. The Humvee has a winch. I can pull it out of the way. Stay here."

"Wait." Alissa leaned forward and grabbed Chris' shoulder. "What if it's an ambush?" Chris thought for a moment. "Kiera, do you know how to use the machine gun?"

"Yes," she replied with way too much enthusiasm.

"Good. If anything comes out of the woods, light them up. Just don't hit me in the crossfire."

Chris waited until Kiera lifted the hatch, climbed into the mount, and had the .50 caliber in her hands before opening the door and stepping out. He listened for any signs of danger. The only sounds came from chirping birds. Moving around to the front of the Humvee, he unwound the cable and pulled it toward the tree, wrapping it twice around the top half and securing it with the hook. Going back to the vehicle, he was about to engage the winch when a rustling to his right made his blood run cold. Chris unslung his AK-47 and moved behind the fender.

Kiera swung the machine gun toward the woods and waited, her finger on the trigger. A few seconds later, a black object pushed through the tree line.

"They're so cute," Kiera cooed.

A family of bears exited the woods onto the road. As the father faced them, staring down the Humvee, the mother bear ushered her three cubs across the asphalt.

"I want to hug them," said Kiera.

"And get mauled?" Chris chuckled, relieved.

Once the bears were safely on the other side of the road, Chris activated the winch. The cable grew taut and pulled the tree sideways. When they had enough room to pass, he stopped. Rushing forward, he detached the hook, switched the winch back on until the cable had been wound around the drum, then quickly climbed back into the Humvee. He drove around the tree and continued their journey.

AS THEY APPROACHED Naples' town limits, Chris slowed down again. "We may have a problem."

A roadblock comprised of two pick-up trucks parked nose to nose stood in the center of the road. A row of spike strips lay across their path one hundred feet ahead of the vehicles. Five men stood guard behind the trucks, each with a stern expression on their face. Three carried shotguns, one an AK-47, and the last an FAL battle rifle. None of the weapons were pointed at the Humvee but could be brought to bear in a second.

Chris stopped in front of the spike strips. A deputy climbed out of a Cumberland County Sheriff Department squad car. He wore a clean, dark brown uniform that strained against his beer belly. His white hair and beard were well groomed. None of the men appeared anxious, indicating they had the situation here under control.

The deputy passed between the pick-ups and approached the driver's side of the Humvee. He slid on a pair of Ray-ban sunglasses and placed his hand on the grip of his pistol. One of the other sentries, a tall man in jeans and a leather jacket who carried the AK-47, joined the deputy and moved around to the passenger's side.

"I'll handle this," said Chris. "Nobody go for your weapons unless I say so."

The side windows on the Humvee were much smaller than a traditional car window, hampering the ability to see inside, so Chris stepped out and left the door open. When the deputy neared, Chris noticed the name Cooper on his name badge. Deputy Cooper stood on the exterior side of the door and scanned the cab, his eyes focusing mainly on the weapons, then made eye contact with Chris. "Is there anything I can do for you folks?"

Chris kept his hands by his side, palms facing the deputy. "We're not looking for any trouble, officer."

"I didn't say you were," Cooper said with all sincerity.

"I noticed you checking out our weapons."

The deputy chuckled. "Son, I'd be more concerned if you were driving around out here without them. Though I must admit, that fifty on the roof is impressive. So, how can I help you?"

"We're just passing through." Chris nodded to Nathan in back. "We have a sick member of the group who the doctors on Warren Island think they can help."

"Warren Island. Isn't that where the military set up a

base?"

Chris nodded. "It is."

Cooper moved around the door. "May I?"

Chris stepped back. "Be my guest. Don't worry about my dog. He barks at everyone."

The deputy leaned inside. Alissa said, "Hello."

"Afternoon, ma'am,"

Shithead barked once, his tail wagging.

"Hey, boy. How you doing?"

Cooper scanned the interior of the Humvee. His eyebrows raised when he saw the stains of blood on Nathan's bandages. "Has your friend been bit?"

Alissa placed a protective hand on Nathan's chest. "He has."

The man with the AK-47 stepped back and raised his weapon when Cooper spoke. "Stand down, Bob. The guy's tied up."

Bob lowered the AK-47. Cooper turned his attention back to Chris. "You know your friend could turn at any minute."

"He was bit two days ago."

Cooper raised his eyebrows again. "Did the medics at Warren Island ask you to bring your friend to them?"

"They did."

Copper thought for a moment. "That makes sense."

"How so?" Alissa asked from the back seat.

"Some of the other towns that have talked with the military said they're looking for people who have been bitten but not affected by the virus. We think they're searching for a vaccine."

Alissa had not thought of that possibility.

"Wait here." Cooper walked around the Humvee and whispered something to Bob, who then went back to the pickups and conversed with the others. Cooper returned to Chris.

"We're going to escort you through town. My men have orders that if anyone emerges near the machine gun or gets out carrying their weapons, they're going to fire on you. Is that clear?"

"Perfectly."

Alissa leaned forward between the front seats. "You mentioned other towns. Will we run into any on our way to the coast?"

"Not if you go straight, ma'am. The only surviving towns are far north of us." Cooper offered his hand. "Best of luck to you. I hope things work out with your friend."

Chris shook it. "Thank you. We appreciate it."

Cooper stepped away from the Humvee. Once Chris had climbed back in and closed the door, the deputy waved. One of the men ran out and pulled the spike strip off the road as the pick-up on the left backed up and headed into town. Chris followed.

Naples was a small town on the banks of Long Lake. They passed a handful of residences and commercial establishments. After a few miles, the pick-up pulled into a gas station and stopped beyond the pumps. Chris followed. Bob exited the passenger side of the truck and approached the Humvee while the driver stepped out, he shotgun at the ready in case he needed to use it.

Chris opened the door and stepped out. "Is anything wrong?"

"Deputy Cooper told me to let you fill up. You'll need all the gas you can to get to the coast safely."

"Thanks."

As Chris filled the tank, Bob moved a few feet away and lit up a cigarette. "Do you want one?"

Chris shook his head.

"Where are you guys coming from?"

"North Conway."

"I heard there was a huge forest fire down there."

"You heard right. Burned the town to the ground plus all the forest around it."

"Damn." Bob took a long drag on the cigarette and exhaled. "You're lucky you survived."

"We almost didn't. Found ourselves caught up in the middle of it." Chris left out the part about battling Dickson's mob and scores of deaders.

Bob took another drag on the cigarette. "Sometimes I wonder if those us who survived are really the lucky ones. I doubt anything will ever return to normal."

"I hope you're wrong. The world can't go on like this forever."

"Amen, brother." Bob pointed toward the Humvee. "God willing your friend in there will be the key to change all this."

The automatic shut-off triggered with a loud clunk. As Chris replaced the nozzle onto the pump, Bob tossed the cigarette on the ground and crushed it out with his foot. "Follow us."

Five minutes later, they reached a causeway over the narrow part of the lake, passed by the marina, and continued to the other end of Naples. Another roadblock lay up ahead. On seeing the Humvee, one of the vans pulled back, allowing them to pass through. One hundred feet beyond the roadblock, Bob jumped out and pulled the spike strip off the road. Chris eased the Humvee forward until Bob waved for him to stop. Chris slid open the window.

"What's up?"

"Did the deputy mention the herd of deaders reported between here and the coast?"

"No, he didn't. Where are they?"

Bob shrugged. "No one knows. We picked up a radio message two days ago from an unidentified group that reported them somewhere near Lewiston. They reported about two hundred deaders traveling in a pack stampeding toward them."

"Stampeding?" asked Chris.

"We figure they must be newly-turned. Probably from a town in central Maine we lost touch with a little over a week ago. We tried getting more info from those who reported the herd, but they never responded. Anyways, be careful out there. And good luck."

Handshakes were exchanged. The pick-up made a U-turn and headed toward town. Chris continued toward the coast.

"Did he say a herd of stampeding deaders?" Kiera asked.

"Yeah." Chris sounded concerned.

"Well, we've been through worse."

"You're kidding?" asked Rebecca.

Kiera proceeded to tell her some of the group's previous adventures.

Alissa ignored the conversation. Instead, she dabbed the sweat from Nathan's head and kissed his brow.

"Don't worry, hon," she whispered in his ear. "We'll get you there safely."

Chapter Six

CHRIS CONTINUED ALONG Route 302 for a few more miles until it intersected with Route 9, then turned north. The farther they traveled, the less populated the area became, which suited everyone fine.

After a few minutes, Rebecca glanced over at Alissa. "What the deputy said back there about a vaccine. Do you think that's possible?"

"If whatever started this outbreak is caused by a virus, then yes."

"That would make it easier to fight them," said Chris. "Being bit wouldn't be a death sentence. We could start taking back what we lost."

Rebecca perked up. "I wonder if we could find a cure."

"God forbid," mumbled Kiera.

Rebecca's cheeriness turned sour. "You don't want to save these people?"

Kiera shifted in the front seat to face Rebecca. "All the deaders are decaying. Bringing them back to life would be inhumane. Not to sound cruel, but they're better off dead."

Rebecca lowered her head. "I never thought about that."

"Besides, I'd hate to think there was a cure. Considering all the deaders I've put down, I wouldn't be able to live with myself if I thought they were only sick and not monsters. It would be like killing cancer patients."

"But...." Rebecca stopped. She had no response.

Alissa rubbed Nathan's forehead. "Can we not talk about

this."

"Yes, please." Chris said it more like an order than a request.

The next fifteen minutes passed in an awkward silence. Kiera broke the quiet, pointing up ahead of them. "What the fuck is that?"

Chris slowed as they approached. A yellow school bus lay on its side along the right shoulder. Blood and gore smeared the undercarriage and the exposed areas of the chassis. The rear emergency door was open. Eight bodies lay behind the bus, six of them stripped clean of flesh, muscles, and organs. The last two had only been partially devoured and had reanimated but were too badly mauled to stand. They dragged their carcasses toward the Humvee.

"What could knock over a school bus?" asked Kiera.

"Maybe the driver lost control," Rebecca answered.

"Or was pushed over by that deader herd," added Chris as he drove past.

Rebecca leaned between the front seats. "We need to stop and see if there are any survivors."

"We don't have the time or the room."

"If there are survivors, we can't abandon them."

Chris shook his head. "We'll radio Naples once we get to Warren Island and they can send a rescue party to check it out. Kiera, what's our location?"

Kiera checked the map. "We're approaching Crockett Corner. We're about at the halfway point."

"Where's Lewiston?"

Kiera checked the map. "Twenty miles to the north."

"Shit," Chris mumbled.

Rebecca turned to Alissa. "Say something."

Alissa glanced down at Nathan. "He's right. We need to proceed as planned."

Knowing when she was defeated, Rebecca crossed her arms over her chest and stared out the window.

THE HUMVEE PASSED through North Yarmouth, another small town abandoned to the living dead, and proceeded to Crockett Corner. Rebecca leaned against her seat and napped. Kiera checked the map as they passed by the golf course to make certain she knew their location. For the hundredth time since leaving the cabin, Alissa felt Nathan's forehead and dabbed away the sweat.

Chris muttered, "Fuck!"

Everyone followed his gaze to the right.

The herd of deaders Bob had warned them about milled on the green to their right, except their numbers were closer to three hundred and fifty. Upon hearing the engine, they turned as one toward the Humvee and charged. Most were freshly reanimated and, as such, approached the vehicle at an alarming speed.

Rebecca slid aside the window in her door and emptied an entire magazine into the stampede. A round struck one deader in the head and a few were toppled by bullets to the leg and crushed by the horde. Her efforts did nothing to slow the rush.

"Should I man the machine gun?" asked Kiera.

"Not enough time." Chris pressed his foot on the accelerator, hoping to out distance the herd. For a few seconds, he thought he could outrun them. He was wrong.

The herd washed across the road like a rogue wave, blocking their path and slamming into the right side of the Humvee. The deaders struck with such force they shoved the Humvee across the road and onto the opposite shoulder. Chris steered back onto the asphalt and kept driving, pushing them aside. Their numbers were too great. Those in front of the vehicle were shoved out of the way or knocked down, the latter getting stuck under the front tires and slowing the Humvee. Within a few seconds, enough deaders piled up that the Humvee climbed up on them and became stuck.

Shifting into reverse, Chris attempted to back off the pile. The rear tires gripped the asphalt, pulling the vehicle off the mass of bodies, and dragging several more beneath it. The Humvee plowed into the deaders behind them, creating another mass of carcasses that the rear wheels became entangled in. The Humvee stopped. Chris tried rocking the vehicle back and forth to break the jam as if he were stuck in deep snow, but only succeeded in digging the wheels deeper into the bodies. Within seconds, all four tires spun like crazy, unable to find traction in the blood and gore. The Humvee was stuck with over three hundred deaders swarming around it, climbing up the hood and onto the roof until those inside the cab could see nothing through the windows but the living dead clawing to get at them.

The stench of decay filtered into the vehicle. Rebecca vomited.

Shithead barked at the deaders through the rear hatch to drive them off, a futile gesture.

Kiera tried to open the hatch to get to the machine gun but the weight of the deaders on the roof prevented her from pushing it aside.

She slumped back into her seat. "What do we do now?"

"What can we do?" asked Rebecca.

"Nothing." Chris' tone dripped with resignation. "We're trapped. Sorry."

Kiera touched his shoulder. "It's not your fault."

"Now we know what happened to the school bus."

"How do we get out of here?" Rebecca was on the verge of panic.

"We don't," said Chris.

"There has to be a way out." A tear flowed down Kiera's cheek.

"There is." Chris withdrew his 1911 from its holster.

"We'll never fight our way through that horde," said Alissa.

"It's not for them." Chris shifted in his seat toward her. "It's for us."

"Y-you can't be serious?" stammered Rebecca.

"What choice do we have? Even if we could get out of here, you saw what happened to those who tried to escape from the bus. I won't let that happen to me."

"Can't we call for help?" asked Kiera.

"The radios are short range. We left them back at the cabin."

"The military will come get us."

"No, they won't," said Alissa. "They're expecting us to come to them. No one knows where we are."

Rebecca clutched at straws. "If we don't show up, they'll come looking for us."

"Or they'll assume we're dead and won't even try. It won't be long before those things break through the glass."

Kiera lowered her head. "I... I can't kill myself. I'll go to Hell."

Chris placed a hand on her shoulder. "I'll take care of that and do myself last, but only if you all agree it's better than being stuck here until we die."

Rebecca shook her head. "I don't know."

From the back, Shithead whimpered, sensing the mood inside the vehicle.

"Alissa?" Chris sought her out for guidance.

Alissa closed her eyes. This was all her fault. Her stupid attempt to save Nathan. Agreeing to let the others go with her. She had led the group to New Hampshire, fought off Dickson's crew, and survived the deader assault on the cabin, only to throw it all away because of her selfishness. She deserved to die, had expected she would not survive this trip. Now she was responsible for sacrificing the lives of her friends. Her mind raced to think of an alternative but could not. Depression and self-loathing clouded her mind.

She opened her eyes and met Chris' gaze. How he must

hate her at this moment. "Let's do it."

"Me first." Kiera lowered her head and closed her eyes.

Chris placed the barrel of the 1911 near her temple and wrapped a finger around the trigger. "God forgive me."

A gunshot rang out.

Chapter Seven

C HRIS LOWERED THE 1911 and stared out the front
window. The head of one of the deaders on the hood
exploded. Its body slid down the windshield, leaving a streak of
congealed blood. A dozen more shots tore into those on the
Humvee, blasting them off. As they fell away, Chris and the
others were able to see ahead of them.

A military unit approached from the north. Three Bradley
fighting vehicles stood in line abreast on Route 9 one thousand
feet ahead of them. Several soldiers stood outside the vehicles,
firing into the herd. When the deaders around the Humvee
turned to attack the new prey, the soldiers fell back into the
Bradleys. The vehicles lurched forward, two moving onto each
shoulder and one pulling into the right lane.

A fourth military vehicle passed the Bradleys. The size of a
tank, it had an angled, spiked mine plow attached to the front
chassis supported by three metallic skies whose pads glided
along the asphalt. As the deaders raced toward it, two rocket-
projected explosive line charges shot out of a launcher mounted
on the turret, sailed through the air for several hundred feet,
and fell amongst the charging herd. A moment later, the twin
lines ignited, a pound of C4 explosives for every linear foot
detonating and ripping apart the living dead. Alissa and the
others watched as chunks of bodies and limbs were thrown up,
falling back to earth in a ghastly rain. The few deaders that
made it through rushed the tank, only to be caught up in the
plow or crushed beneath its treads.

Only a handful of deaders survived the onslaught, almost all of them still surrounding the Humvee. Two of the Bradleys rolled up alongside the Humvee and the third took up a position to its rear. As the troops inside used the firing ports to clear the deaders around the Humvee, the three Bradleys opened fire with their 25mm cannons and co-axial 7.62 machine guns on the slower ones in the distance still stumbling toward the fray, ripping them apart within seconds.

"Fucking awesome." Kiera high-fived Chris.

The Bradleys pulled away and stopped, forming a triangular formation around the Humvee with their turrets facing to the flanks. Four Stryker armored personnel carriers pulled in between the Bradleys. Nine soldiers rushed out of the back of each carrier and spread out as they approached, shooting in the head the few deaders still moving. In a matter of seconds, it was all over. The herd had been eliminated, leaving behind a blood-soaked killing field.

A sergeant with the name NOWACK stitched onto his uniform breastplate stepped up and waved at the driver's window. "It's all clear. You can come out."

Chris opened the door. The nauseating stench of decayed flesh mixed with the odor of ruptured gastrointestinal systems wafted through the cabin. The Humvee rested several feet off the ground on a mound of corpses. Chris lowered himself to the road, careful not to trip over the bodies or slip on the blood and gore. The others joined him. Shithead jumped from the back onto Alissa's seat, careful not to step on Nathan, and exited the vehicle. Running over to the nearest shattered body, he raised his right rear leg and peed on it.

Nowack chuckled, but quickly suppressed it and restored a professional demeanor. "If you'll follow me, the captain wants to talk to you."

Alissa and the others waded through the carnage. The soldiers moved amongst the bodies, finding it difficult to not step on a corpse or body part, shooting in the head any deaders that showed signs of life.

As they approached the lead Stryker, an officer with silver bars on a tab hanging over the top of his body armor issued orders to his team leads. When the last soldier saluted and left, Nowack stepped forward.

"Captain, these are the people from inside the Humvee."

He turned to face Alissa and the others. He was tall, just under six feet, with a thin but muscular physique. Alissa thought he appeared too young to be a captain until she noticed a few streaks of grey in his blonde hair. Like his men, the captain was well groomed and fed, and wore a fresh uniform. He held a lit cigar in his right hand, already burned down to the end.

"I'm Captain Jonathon West, Maine National Guard, 521st Troop Command. Are you the people we talked to by radio yesterday?"

Chris nodded. "The same."

"Which one of you is Alissa?"

"That's me."

West switched his cigar to his left hand and extended his right. "It's a pleasure to meet you."

"Thank you." Alissa shook the captain's hand and introduced the other members of her group.

With the greeting done, West switched the cigar back to his right hand and took a puff. "You people have caused quite a buzz at Islesboro."

"How so?" asked Alissa.

"Because of your friend who was bitten but hasn't turned. The medical team on our compound are hoping his blood can be used to create a vaccine."

"Is that even possible?"

"You mean creating a vaccine?" The captain shrugged and puffed on his cigar. "You'd have to ask the doctors and scientists back at base. They think it's a possibility. I hope they can. I'm tired of losing my men to this damn outbreak."

"Not that I'm complaining," said Alissa. "But how did you know we needed help?"

"We assumed you might. Early this morning, we picked up radio chatter about a herd of runners in the area you said you'd be traveling through. Sparks called your cabin but you had already left and your people had no way of contacting you. I figure it couldn't hurt to meet you halfway. I'm glad we found you in time."

"Us, too," said Chris.

Shithead barked.

"Where's your friend?"

Alissa motioned to the Humvee. "In the back."

"I'm transferring you to the Strykers. You'll be safer that way, especially when we get back to the perimeter. You and your friend can ride with me in the lead. The women can follow in the one behind us."

"What about the Humvee?"

"I'm having some of my men pull it off the mound of dead. My team will drive it back for you." West puffed on the cigar. "Is there anything you need while we transfer your friend?"

Chris pointed to the tank-like vehicle. "What's that thing?'

"It's an M1150 Assault Breacher Vehicle. We use them to clean out minefields in Iraq. This one had yet to be deployed when the outbreak began, which turned out to be lucky for us. You saw her in action. She's great at taking out the living dead. We've needed her because of the situation at Warren Island."

Alissa raised her eyebrows. "What situation is that?"

"It's nothing to worry about, but you'll see for yourself soon enough."

Sergeant Nowack came up to the captain. "Their friend is being transferred to your Stryker."

"Excellent. Round up everyone and let's get out of here." West took a long, final draw on his cigar and tossed it onto a pile of deader corpses before turning to Alissa and the others. "We should be back at base in a few hours."

"Thanks," answered Alissa. "We'd like that."

Chapter Eight

I T TOOK A little over two hours for the convoy to reach their destination. The unit stayed on back roads, crossing I-95 several miles south of Augusta, then picked up Route 17 until they reached the coastal town of Rockport. After that, it was a brief run up Route 1 to Lincolnville, their destination. The few deaders the military had encountered on the way to rescue Alissa's group had already been eliminated, not that anyone inside the Stryker could see the carnage since the vehicle lacked windows.

Chris rested his head against the steel bulkhead and napped with Shithead at his feet, wide awake and his tail wagging constantly at the thrill of going for a ride. Alissa sat opposite them, her attention focused on Nathan, wishing they would arrive soon. She desperately wanted him to get medical attention. His condition remained the same, but deep down she knew every hour that passed worsened his chances of recovery. No one spoke during the trip back to Warren Island, which suited Alissa. After nearly getting all of them killed, she did not feel like engaging in conversation.

The driver notified West they were approaching the ferry area.

"Any deaders?" he asked.

"Just a handful. Nothing to be concerned about."

"Excellent. You know the procedure." West turned to Alissa's group. "Anyone interested in taking a look?"

"I am," said Chris, who woke up from his nap.

The captain scooted to his right and pointed to the hatch above his head. "Be my guest."

Chris climbed up and poked his upper body through the opening. Ahead of them stood a makeshift barricade, each wall comprised of two adjacent rows of ten containers, double stacked. The ends of the outer walls extended fifteen feet into the ocean. Poles had been welded along the top of the wall with five barbed wire strands running between them. Five-foot-long metal spikes had been inserted at two-foot intervals into a mound of concrete around the perimeter. More than a dozen deaders were imbedded on the spikes, most having died of starvation and rotted away, a few still reanimated and clutching at the metal walls in front of them.

As the convoy passed the wall, it turned off Route One onto McKay Road. A trench ten feet wide and fifty feet long had been dug out of the ground in front of the gate to trap any of the living dead trying to gain access. Seven deaders sauntered around the entrance. As the convoy approached, the gate lowered, revealing itself to be a draw bridge like those used in Medieval castles, only this one was made of corrugated metal supported by steel girders. The draw bridge crushed two deaders under its weight. Four more were taken down by gunfire from guards posted on top of the containers. The convoy passed over the bridge into a concrete parking lot. A bulldozer sat to the side of the opening, its engine idling. Once the last vehicle had crossed over, the military raised the draw bridge. The last deader had followed behind the convoy, being caught in the middle of the bridge as it swung up. It tumbled off the ramp into the compound. The bulldozer surged forward, crushing the deader beneath its tracks.

Ahead of them stood two docks, one small with a single motor board anchored alongside. The larger dock led to a car ferry that had its ramp lowered. As the three Bradleys and three Strykers drove on to the ferry, the M1150 pulled into a U-turn to the right and parked in the center of the lot. Once the other vehicles were aboard, a soldier raised the ramp. A minute later, the ferry set off across the bay for Warren Island.

Chris lowered himself back into the Stryker. "Impressive."

"Thanks," said West. "It took the Army Corps of Engineers three weeks to set that up. It wasn't easy. Back then, we had a constant stream of deaders trying to get to the dock. Now we get no more than a handful a day. Follow me."

The captain made his way to the rear of the Stryker, lowered the vehicle's ramp, and exited on to the ferry. Alissa and Chris followed, joined by Kiera and Rebecca from the other APC. He led them to the bow.

"That's Warren Island. We made base camp at Islesboro. The locals weren't happy at first. They thought we were commandeering the island from them. They changed their minds when the outbreak reached this far north. Now they're grateful for the protection, although no deaders have made it out there."

"Why didn't you set up at one of the local military bases?" asked Alissa.

"Too dangerous." West pulled a cigar from his pocket and bit off the end. "All the bases were overrun in a matter of days, mostly because civilians flocked to them for safety. Some were infected. The virus spread rapidly. Warren Island is the perfect location because it's completely isolated. No causeways to the mainland. The only way onto the island is by the ferry or a private airstrip up north, and we locked that down on day one. Anyone wanting to come to the island must undergo a full body search to make certain they haven't been bitten and then spend twenty-four hours in quarantine back at the terminal. This is the only safe haven around for two hundred miles."

"How many people are here?" asked Rebecca.

"A little over two thousand. One hundred and eighteen are military. The rest are locals and refugees." West placed the cigar between his teeth and lit it. "We have it good. We set up living quarters in the local school, which is solar powered, so the civilians have heat, plumbing, and electricity. We get supplied twice a week, so no one is going without food or water, although the menu is mostly MREs. Dr. Carrington set up a lab at the local clinic where he and the other scientists have been trying to find a vaccine for the deader virus, so far without success. That's why they're so interested in your friend. Hopefully, we can find a way to cure him and put an end to this nightmare."

"Thanks." Alissa forced a smile. "Any idea what caused the outbreak?"

The captain puffed on the cigar and blew out a cloud of bluish-white smoke. "Not a clue. At first, we thought it might have been an attack by terrorists or some radical group trying to topple capitalism. But the outbreak occurred around the world at the same time. The only countries capable of pulling off such a feat, like China and Russia, have also been ravaged by the virus, so we've ruled out a man-made incident. Scientists from all over the world are stymied."

"You're in touch with other countries?"

"Only Japan, South Korea, China, Israel, and several countries in Europe. Everywhere else has gone dark."

"How bad is the situation around the world?" asked Kiera.

"As bad as it is here in the States, or worse." West puffed on his cigar. "Unfortunately for the Saudis, they were in the middle of Ramadan when the outbreak struck, and more people were in Mecca than usual celebrating the Hajj. Mecca fell in less than twenty-four hours and the peninsula within a week. The Chinese nuked Beijing, Shanghai, and several other cities with load-grade weapons to check the spread, without success. Russia tried to quarantine Moscow but the deaders overran their defenses within days."

"What about islands?" asked Chris.

"Same as the mainland. The greater the population, the quicker it fell. Ships at sea suffered outbreaks. We lost contact with more than half our naval vessels, and other countries have reported the same. There were reports of the virus reaching some of the outposts in Antarctica, though the crews there were able to contain it and quarantine the infected. The only places that fared well are isolated regions like the northern states near the Canadian border, Siberia, Australia's outback, and central Africa. Except for a few isolated towns, we've lost contact with everything west of the Rockies and east of the Mississippi."

"Dear God." Alissa sighed. "What about the government?"

"Few made it out of Washington alive. The Speaker of the House is in charge from New Mexico."

"What's in New Mexico?"

"The White Sands Missile Range outside of Albuquerque. It's secure with no one around for hundreds of square miles. We tried to get her to NORAD in Colorado, but she refused to be stuck underground in case an outbreak occurred there. Not that I can blame her. It turned out to be a good thing. We lost touch with NORAD three weeks ago."

No one said anything. It was hard enough taking in the information they just received.

As they approached the ferry terminal on Warren Island, everyone moved back into their vehicles. Once on land, it took only a few minutes for the convoy to drive to the hospital. The back ramp of the Stryker lowered, revealing a team of doctors and nurses ready to take Nathan to the Emergency Room. West ordered everyone out. As they waited in the parking lot, the medical team entered the vehicle, transferred Nathan to a stretcher, and wheeled him into the Emergency Room. One of the doctors broke away from the others and walked over to the civilians. Of average height and build, he appeared to be in his mid-forties, an image belied by the streaks of grey in his dark hair and the five-day growth of stubble on his face. His demeanor indicated he was in charge.

"This is Dr. Carrington," West introduced him. "He's the head of our research team."

"Not that we've accomplished much," the doctor replied

42

with humility. "Which of you is Alissa?"

Alissa stepped forward. "I am."

"I'm so glad you made it." The doctor offered his hand. "We were worried when we heard about the runners in the area."

"Don't remind us," said Chris. Shithead barked in agreement.

"I promise, we'll take good care of your friend."

"I'd like to stay with him," pleaded Alissa.

"You can if you like, but we have to run a series of tests on him and start an antibiotic regimen. It's going to be hectic in there for a few hours. I can put you all up in beds in the hospital while you wait. I'll call you the minute he's able to have visitors or if there's a change in his condition."

"I don't want to leave him."

Rebecca placed a hand on Alissa's shoulders. "I'll stay nearby in case Nathan wakes up. You need to rest."

Alissa hesitated.

"It's for the best," said Carrington. "I promise we'll take good care of him and will call you once he's ready."

"Kiera and I will stay with you," offered Chris.

Alissa caved in. "Okay."

Carrington nodded and turned to a nurse who hovered nearby. "Marie, take our guests to rooms 109 and 110. Make certain they have anything they desire."

"Yes, doctor." The nurse stepped forward. "Will you follow me, please?"

As Carrington and Rebecca set off toward the Emergency Room, Marie led the others to their rooms.

Chapter Nine

T HE LAST THING Alissa needed was to be by herself. She lay in the hospital bed and stared out the window. Even though exhausted, she could not sleep. She had wanted to be with Nathan as much as to keep her mind preoccupied as to be with her lover if he needed her. Now, alone with her thoughts, her mind kept replaying the events of the past few days, feeding off the guilt and sense of stupidity welling up inside her.

And shame.

Sure, Alissa was proud of everything she had done for the group up until now. More like a feeling of accomplishment. Helping other people had always been a calling for her. In school, she used to the protect weaker kids from the assholes when she caught them being bullied in the halls and play-ground. In college, she had volunteered for the Red Cross and the campus clinic. Coming to the need of others had been in her blood as far back as she could remember. Everything she had down over the past few months had been part of her nature. Nothing had changed in that respect, except now she did it during a deader apocalypse.

What had changed was her being the leader of the group. It still amazed her how she had fallen into that role. She had always been there to help others, not oversee the efforts. Nathan would have made a better leader with his years of experience as a police officer. Steve and Miriam had good heads on their shoulders and would have done fine. Even Chris would have done a good job. Well, maybe not Chris. He was a bit of a loose cannon, although she did admire that he came to help them when the deaders attacked the cabin rather than keep himself safe. If it hadn't been for him, they'd all be dead. Still, each of them was as qualified as her to lead the group, if not more so. Why did they turn to her for guidance?

That would probably change after today. She had been foolhardy in her effort to get Nathan medical attention, letting her heart guide her rather than common sense. She should have realized that the scientists wanted to study Nathan as much as she wanted him to get better and allowed the military to come get them. They were more than capable of doing so, as today proved. Instead, she let her emotions get in the way and her recklessness nearly got all of them killed.

Two things bothered her more than being in charge. The first was encouraging Kiera to go with them on every mission. Yes, Kiera acted mature for her age and made a great deader hunter. Kiera had saved the lives of Little Stevie and Connie during the deader attack on the cabin. And Archer. However, the girl was only fourteen. She still played video games with her brother. Granted, due to the outbreak she would never live the life of a normal teenager. Still, Alissa had shown incredible irresponsibility in putting Kiera in harm's way. If… when they got back to the cabin, she would put an end to such foolishness and apologize to Miriam. Thankfully, nothing bad had happened to Kiera so far.

What bothered Alissa most was agreeing to the suicide pact they had made in the Humvee. She had no idea what possessed her to go along with it. Again, for some reason they looked to her for guidance and she nearly fucked them over. Kiera had been seconds away from being killed due to her. If the military had not shown up when they did…. Alissa could not bear to imagine what would have happened. She should have recommended they wait until the situation got worse, at least tried to keep them alive rather than take the easy way out. One of them would have figured a way out of their situation. The incident proved her incapable of being in charge. When this was over, she would pass on the reigns of command to someone else. Getting rid of her guilt and shame over what had nearly transpired would stay with Alissa the rest of her life.

Rolling onto her side, Alissa buried her face into the pillow and cried.

She did not hear Rebecca enter the room a few minutes later. "Are you all right?"

Alissa raised her head, composed herself, and wiped the snot and tears from her face before getting up. "Sorry. I didn't want anyone to see me like this."

"That's okay," said Rebecca. "Even Jesus wept."

"Jesus saved lives."

"So do you. Everyone in our group is alive today thanks to you."

Alissa did not want to argue that point. "Is everything okay with Nathan?"

"He's fine and is resting comfortable. Dr. Carrington asked me to come get you."

Alissa took a deep breath, held it for ten seconds, and slowly exhaled. The exercise did little to ease her anxiety and sense of uselessness, but it did clear her mind.

"I'm ready."

ALISSA'S HEART SOARED when she saw Nathan. He rested comfortably in the ER bed. His hands, legs, and head were restrained to the side rails and headboard by leather straps. She took the IV drip in his right arm as a good sign. It meant the doctors had not given up hope for him. She moved over to check the bags. In addition to a saline solution to keep him hydrated and lower his temperature, he also received Fluoro-quinolones, the most powerful antibiotic available. Alissa felt his forehead. Nathan no longer sweated and his brow seemed cooler.

"His temperature has dropped," she said to no one in particular.

"The last reading fifteen minutes ago was 100.6." Carrington stood in the doorway. "We were lucky. The infection was caused by the bacteria in the bite wound and not the virus."

"So, he'll live?"

"You're a nurse, so you know as well as I do that things could change for the worst. But, if your friend keeps going at this rate, he should make a full recovery in a few weeks."

"Thank you, doctor."

"You're welcome. You're free to stay with him if you like."

"I do." Alissa bent forward, kissing Nathan on the forehead.

She shifted her attention back to Carrington. "Will you be able to produce a vaccine from his blood?"

The doctor's expression soured. "Unfortunately, no. We found active traces of the deader virus in his blood. It's impossible to tell yet if he's fighting only the infection or the virus as well. My people are working on his blood now to see if they can develop a cure. We've been focusing on a vaccine, so it's not going to be easy switching gears, especially with our limited resources."

"I'm sorry."

"It's not your fault. What we need is someone uninfected by a deader bite."

The realization struck Alissa like a hammer strike. "I know where we can find one."

Chapter Ten

TEN MINUTES LATER, Alissa and Carrington sat in Colonel Christopher Williams' headquarters in the elementary school where his troops bunked. Williams, the commanding officer of the 521st, had taken over the principal's office, the only change having been made being the clearing of the desk. It seemed strange to see the posters on the wall, one urging kids to throw kindness like confetti, one assuring the kids that if they're failing it means they're trying, and one of the ubiquitous kitten clawing desperately to the end of a rope with the worn out phrase "Hang in There, Baby." The shelf to the colonel's right contained books on education and a series of novels designed for grade schoolers. A frame on the top shelf showed a handsome man in his mid-thirties hugging an equally attractive woman at Disneyland. Two children, about the same age as Kiera and Little Stevie, stood in front of them and smiled. Alissa could not help but wonder if they were among the survivors finding sanctuary on the island or wandering around the mainland as part of the living dead.

"Let me get this straight," said Williams. "You're telling me know where we can get blood from a bite victim who was not infected?"

"I do. On the first day of the outbreak, while trying to escape from Mass General, I ran into a doctor who had been bitten. He asked me to take him to the pathology lab and draw blood samples, saying it was important. At the time I was too busy staying alive to understand what he meant, but now I realize he wanted me to store his blood for a possible vaccine."

"You're certain he'd been bit?"

Alissa nodded. "His abdomen had been ripped open and fed on by a deader. That's how he died. He bled out."

"And he showed no signs of reanimating?" asked Carrington.

"None. I kept a gun trained on him waiting for him to turn, but he never did."

The doctor grew excited. "This could be the break we're looking for."

Williams thought for a few moments. "Where are the samples?"

"I had two of them on me but a deader ripped away the backpack and I lost them."

"Damn it," said Carrington. "Even if we found the backpack, the blood would have gone bad by now."

"I also stored two vials in the refrigerator in the lab." Alissa looked between the two men. "They should still be good."

"Assuming the electricity is on," snorted the colonel.

"It should be. The hospital's emergency power system runs on solar energy."

"It's the best chance we have," pushed Carrington. "We've never encountered anyone who has been bitten and not reanimated."

"What about their friend?"

Carrington shook his head. "He has traces of the virus in him. We hopefully can use his blood to develop a cure, not a vaccine."

"How do we know this guy in Boston didn't get infected with the virus and had been fighting it?"

"We don't," admitted the doctor. "But right now, it's our only hope of producing a vaccine."

Williams focused on Alissa. "What's the situation like at Mass General?"

Alissa suppressed a shiver as she remembered that day. "It's a nightmare. The outbreak started in the ER and spread through the hospital. As far as I know, I'm the only who made it out. Barely."

"You're absolutely certain about everything you told me?"

"Yes." Every event of that first day had been seared into her memory.

"Enough to bet your life on it?"

"Yes."

The colonel leaned forward, resting his elbows on the desk. "Good. I'll arrange for a team to go in and retrieve the samples. You'll escort them."

Alissa felt her bladder want to drain. "No fucking way I'm going back there."

"Ma'am, I understand that I'm asking a lot of you—"

"I almost died in there. I… I can't go back."

"You know the layout of the hospital. You know where the lab is and how to get in. You also know which blood samples to take."

Panic started to overwhelm Alissa. "I'll draw a map."

"I understand your anxiety about going back." The colonel spoke in a soft, soothing tone. "The fact remains that without you, my people stand minimal chance of success."

"What are the odds if I do go?"

"Fifty-fifty."

"That's not very encouraging."

"I know. I can't order you in. The choice is yours."

Carrington jumped in. "Without that blood sample, we have no way of stopping this."

Alissa knew he was right. "That's not fair."

"This whole damn apocalypse isn't fair."

Alissa could not refuse but still sought a way out. "How will we get there? The city and the surrounding suburbs are overrun with deaders."

"We'll fly you in," said Williams.

"I thought you didn't have any aircraft?"

"We don't. But the *Iwo Jima* is sailing off the coast. It's an amphibious assault ship which has helicopters aboard. They've spent the last two months rescuing survivors. One of their choppers will fly you to Mass General, land on the roof, and fly you back once you've retrieved the samples."

"When do we go?"

"I'll check with the captain of the *Iwo Jima*. If not tomorrow morning, then the day after."

No one spoke. Each of them knew the potential gains outweighed the risks involved. Alissa accepted the inevitable. Maybe this would turn out to be her redemption for almost getting the others killed.

Carrington broke the silence. "Come on. I'll take you back to Nathan."

Chapter Eleven

A LISSA STAYED WITH Nathan all afternoon to spend time with him before she left for Boston, though little of it was spent alone. Every fifteen minutes, one of the nurses on duty would come in to check on his vital signs and change his IV when necessary. Twice, a lab technician arrived to take more blood samples. Sergeant Nowack dropped by to inform Alissa that the *Iwo Jima* would send a helicopter to pick them up at 0700. It came as no surprise that, right after dinner, the rest of the group popped by.

Rebecca handed Alissa a Styrofoam tray. "We brought you something from the mess hall."

"Thanks. What is it?"

Chris grinned. "Shit on a shingle."

"What?"

Rebecca rolled her eyes. "Cream chipped beef on toast."

"It doesn't sound appetizing." Alissa placed the container on the floor.

"It's good," chimed in Kiera and reached down to pet the dog's ear. "Shithead loved it."

"That's not a five-star recommendation." Alissa chuckled for the first time in three days.

At that moment, Marie entered to take her quarter-hour reading of Nathan. She paused at the end of the bed. "What is that mangy thing doing here?"

"Lighten up," said Chris. "Kiera doesn't look that bad."

Kiera turned to Chris, placed her fists together in front of her face, and used an imaginary crank in her right hand to slowly raise the middle finger of her left.

The nurse sighed and continued with her job. "You're lucky the colonel told us to cut you some slack because you're VIPs otherwise I'd throw out the lot of you." She turned to Alissa. "Except you, hon. Can I get in there?"

"Sure. We'll talk in the hall."

"Thanks."

Once in the hall, Rebecca said, "We heard you're heading into Boston tomorrow to retrieve blood samples that could provide a vaccine against the virus."

The statement shocked Alissa. "How do know that?"

"This is a military base," said Chris. "The only thing that spreads faster than the deader virus are rumors."

"Is it true?" asked Kiera.

"It is. While escaping from the hospital, I ran into a doctor who had been bitten and died from his wounds, but never reanimated. He had me take samples of his blood and store them in a laboratory fridge. Carrington thinks they can generate a vaccine from that."

"That's wonderful news." Rebecca hugged Alissa. "Once again, you're a hero."

"Thanks." Alissa forced a smile. The last thing she felt like was a hero.

"I'm going with you," said Chris.

"Me, too," Kiera added excitedly.

Alissa made eye contact with the teenager. "You're not going!"

"Why not?"

"It's too dangerous."

"How is this any different?"

"Because I said so."

"That's not fair," Kiera whined.

"Listen to me, young lady. You're a kid and I'm an adult. You'll do as I tell you."

The expression of hurt on Kiera's face quickly morphed into anger. Spinning around, she left the group and stormed out of the hospital into the parking lot.

"I'll check on her." Rebecca excused herself and went after Kiera.

Shithead glanced up at Chris and whimpered.

"Go ahead, boy."

The dog trotted after the two women.

"What's gotten into you?"

Alissa did not feel the need to explain herself. "You're not going, either."

"Excuse me?"

"You heard me," Alissa snapped, then immediately moderated her tone. "Sorry. I don't mean to be a bitch. I've already put enough people in danger. Not this time. It's a suicide mission."

"All the more reason I should go."

"I have to go. I'm the only one who knows where the pathology lab is and which blood samples to retrieve. I don't want to put any of you in danger."

"In case you forgot, it's the apocalypse. We're in danger every single day of our lives." Alissa tried to speak, but Chris cut her off. "I understand you not wanting to take Kiera along. But let's be honest, the military's main priority is bringing those samples back safely. You need someone whose priority is getting you back. I'm going. End of discussion."

Alissa was on two minds whether to punch Chris or hug him. She opted for the latter and threw her arms around his neck. "Thank you. But if you get killed, I'm never speaking to you again."

"Don't worry." Chris did not break the hug. "If anything happens to me, though, I'm coming back to haunt you."

"Deal." Alissa broke the embrace. "We're leaving at 0700."

"I'll be there. I'll leave you alone with Nathan. Just promise me you'll get some sleep. You'll need it for tomorrow."

"I will." Alissa knew that would be difficult. Ever since agreeing to accompany the team into Boston, she could not repress the nightmares of what she had endured at the hospital.

"I'm going to check on Kiera. If I know her, she's probably kicking the shit out of one of the Humvees in the parking lot."

"Thanks. See you in the morning." Alissa watched Chris as he made his way outside, deep down glad he would be there.

Marie exited Nathan's room. "All set, hon. You can go back inside. Let me know if you need anything."

"I will."

Alissa entered the room. She pulled the recliner the staff had brought into the room over to the bed. Stretching out, she took Nathan's hand and tried to get some sleep.

THE NIGHT DRAGGED by. As Alissa had anticipated, between the nurses coming in every fifteen minutes and her own fears and anxieties, she had gotten only fitful naps throughout the evening. She was glad when the first rays of sunlight burst through the hospital window.

Chris entered the room. "I assume you didn't get any sleep."

"Not much."

"It's 6:30. There's a driver waiting outside to take us to the airfield."

Alissa stood, stretched her aching muscles, and pushed the recliner back against the wall. Before leaving, she bent over and kissed Nathan on the forehead, whispering in his ear, "I'll be back soon."

Sergeant Nowack waited outside in a Humvee. As they climbed in, Alissa saw Rebecca and Shithead sitting in back. "Where's Kiera?"

"She's still mad at you."

"Mad?" said Chris from the back seat. "She's as pissed as a

wet raccoon with rabies."

Alissa lowered her head. "I shouldn't have yelled at her."

"She'll get over it," said Rebecca.

"I wish she were here. I wanted to apologize."

Chris leaned forward and patted her shoulder. "You can when we get back."

They drove north for several minutes until they reached the airstrip. Nowack stopped by the terminal and everyone got out. Ten minutes later, the thudding of rotor blades came from the southeast. A Sikorsky SH-60 Seahawk helicopter appeared on the horizon, approaching low over the buildings. Once over the landing strip, it hovered for several seconds before descending, settling on its landing gear. The troop door slid open and the crew chief jumped out, ducked beneath the rotors, and ran over to the others. He removed his helmet. "I'm Mark Bellemah. Are you the civilians we're picking up?"

"We are," said Alissa. "Give us a moment, please."

Rebecca stepped up and hugged Alissa. "I'll look after Nathan until you get back."

"Thank you."

"You two take care of yourselves."

Shithead followed his master toward the chopper. Chris turned around. "You can't go with me, boy."

The dog stopped.

"You keep Rebecca safe."

Shithead moved closer to Chris. "No."

Rebecca crouched and patted her leg. "Come here, Shithead."

Bellamah raised an eyebrow. "Shithead?"

Chris grinned. "You'd understand if you knew him."

Shithead took a few steps toward Rebecca, paused, and looked back at his master. Chris motioned for him to go with Rebecca, which he did, a forlorn expression on his face.

"Follow me, please," said Bellemah.

He led them back to the Seahawk, ushered them inside,

and closed the troop door. As he handed out helmets and secured them in their seats, the pilot shifted to greet them and removed his helmet, revealing a blonde crew cut. The officer was young, attractive, and confident.

"I'm Lieutenant Sam Robson. The gentleman beside me is First Lieutenant Paul Frank. We'll be your chauffeurs this morning."

"Will champagne be served on this flight?" joked Chris.

"Sorry, sir. We ran out. A supply and demand issue. But I do have some lukewarm faucet water in a military canteen if that's to your liking."

"It'll do."

A few minutes later, they were airborne and heading southwest.

ALISSA HAD RIDDEN in helicopters before, all of them medical evac choppers that provided way more comfort than this. Her grandfather always joked about how the military was great at efficiency but sucked at luxury. Now she understood what he meant. The Seahawk had been built for combat. The cabin was cold, the seats uncomfortable, and the noise from the engine loud. It made for an unpleasant forty-five minutes that seemed like hours.

Robson's voice came through the helmets. "Our destination is off to starboard."

Alissa and Chris moved closer to stare out the right window. They flew four hundred feet above the surface. Below them, a naval vessel that looked like a small version of an aircraft carrier sailed toward them. No other vessels accompanied it, not that any were necessary. The only threat now came from a dead enemy and not an opposing navy. Only a handful of aircraft sat on the flight deck – two Harrier II attack aircraft parked near the stern, three Bell Super Cobra attack helicopters and a Marine Corps Bell UH-1Y utility helicopter by the island, and one more Seahawk on the bow.

Robson maneuvered the helicopter behind the vessel, banked into a turn, and approached from the stern. A sailor in a white vest, the Landing Signal Officer, directed the helicopter over the flight deck and, when centered above the landing zone, motioned for it to descend. The landing gear touched down, slightly jostling those inside. Robson shut down the engines, removed his helmet, and leaned toward the back.

"Welcome to the luxury liner *Iwo Jima*. The buffet opens at noon. Today's special is whatever the cook can find in the kitchen. Backgammon is available on the bow near the anti-aircraft guns. Our crew has prepared spacious cots for you in the Marines' quarters. We know you had no choice of airlines, but we thank you for flying Miracle Air. Remember our motto: If you get there, it's a miracle."

Chris laughed. Alissa rolled her eyes.

Bellamah opened the hatch. Alissa and Chris stepped out onto the deck of the *Iwo Jima*.

Chapter Twelve

AN OFFICER DRESSED in a tan uniform, the gold star and double bars of an ensign pinned to his collars, approached. He stood a little over six feet in height, burly, with dark hair and a beard tinted with white from the stress of command. The stern visage morphed into a friendly smile as he extended his hand.

"Ensign Paul Simon."

"Alissa Madison." She shook the hand. His grip was firm but not domineering.

"Chris Kelly." He also shook the ensign's hand.

"It's a pleasure to have you aboard. Well, maybe not a pleasure, not under these circumstances. But the crew will do anything we can to accommodate you until we arrive in Boston."

"When will that be?" asked Alissa.

"Approximately ninety minutes. The captain wants the *Iwo Jima* to be in the harbor when you lift off, that way we can provide a distraction and draw some of the heat away from your team."

"Who is our team?"

"You'll be meeting them in an hour. Captain Frank Gibson is heading up the retrieval team. He's the best we have. Did ten tours in Iraq and Afghanistan plus led a few covert ops that I don't even know the details about. If anyone can get you in and out unharmed, it'll be the major. His team is being briefed on the current deader situation in Boston. Once they're done, the captain wants to talk with you both. Until then, you have the run of the ship."

Chris raised an eyebrow. "I could use a few cups of coffee and something to eat."

"I'll have one of the crew show you to the mess hall." Simon turned to Alissa. "And you, ma'am?"

"If it's okay with you, I'd like to stay here and wander the deck, clear my head a bit."

"I can't allow that, ma'am. Buy if you come with me, I'll have one of the Marines escort you to the fantail."

"That'll be fine. Thank you."

Simon led Alissa and Chris back to the island.

THE FIRST FORTY-FIVE minutes of the voyage had been pleasant, despite having a Marine hover within fifteen feet of Alissa the entire time on the fantail. The sounds of the ocean sliding along the side of the ship comforted her. For the first time in days, her concerns and self-recrimination no longer dominated her thoughts. She remembered the good times, like the cruise she and Paul had taken on their honeymoon, and the time the two of them had made love late at night on their back deck, their sounds of passion mixing with the roar of the waves. She wondered where Paul was now and prayed he had survived.

She had always loved the ocean. In the good weather, she had kept the windows open at night to hear the waves lapping the shore behind her house. On stressful days, and there were quite a few of those being an ER nurse, she would relax on her back deck and read as she sipped a glass of wine, more often than not putting the book aside to enjoy the view. The ocean had always relaxed her. Alissa hoped it would have the same effect now.

Then the ship passed Nahant and the memories of those

first few days following the outbreak swarmed her thoughts. Flashbacks filtered in about the fall of the island, the struggle she and Nathan had to make it through the town, and their near catastrophe at the dock when they boarded Steve's boat and escaped the carnage. And, of course, the nightmare of watching the last few survivors attempting to escape the deaders. Self-doubt washed over her again like a flood tide.

"Are you all right?" asked a voice from behind her.

She glanced over her shoulder. Chris approached, also accompanied by a Marine escort. He handed her a bottle of water. "I thought you could use this."

"Thanks, but I'm not thirsty."

"You're the one always telling the rest of us to stay hydrated. Are you going to be one of those nurses who doesn't follow her own advice?"

Alissa took the bottle, twisted off the cap, and drank half the bottle in one gulp to placate Chris. She did need to drink but refused to admit it.

"Thanks."

"You're welcome." Chris gazed out and saw Nahant. "Maybe we should go below."

"I'm fine," she lied. "I prefer it here. We'll be trapped inside soon enough."

"Are you sure you're okay with going back to Mass General?"

"I have no choice. Besides, I'll be fine as long as you're with me."

He smiled. An awkward moment passed when Alissa thought he might try to kiss her.

Thankfully, the approach of a female Marine interrupted the tense situation.

"Are you Alissa and Chris?"

"We are."

"I'm Gunnery Sergeant Chell Lynn Dobyns. I'm one of the team who'll be escorting you back to the hospital. The captain wants to talk with you."

"Lead the way." Alissa walked around Chris and joined the gunnery sergeant. Chris fell in behind her, followed by their escorts.

THE REST OF the team – Captain Gibson and three more Marines – were waiting when they arrived in the ready room. Upon seeing the new arrivals, the captain stepped forward to greet them. A three-day growth of beard covered his face accompanied by a full head of dark hair. A thick strand draped across his forehead. He pushed it back into place with his right hand.

"You must be Miss Madison and Mr. Kelly."

"Please, call us Alissa and Chris."

"Roger that. I'm Captain Frank Gibson. I'll be leading the mission to retrieve the blood samples. You've already met Gunnery Sergeant Dobyns. This is the rest of the team. Corporal Steven Overturf."

A young man looked up. Alissa guessed him to be in his mid-twenties although months of combat against the deaders had resulted in crow's feet around the eyes. The corporal flashed Alissa a smile equal parts arrogance and confidence. "You've fought with the rest, now you fight with the best."

"Private First Class Michael Foster."

The sullen teenager offered a half wave. Short and lanky, and wearing thick glasses, he appeared the opposite of what one would imagine of a Marine.

"And Private Gail Hoak."

The private, an attractive woman with toned muscles and blonde hair buzzed short, sneered. "Are these the civilians we're babysitting?"

"Can it, Hoak," snapped Gibson. "This lady fought her way out of a hospital and a city overrun by deaders and has survived three months on her own. She's probably encountered more deaders than all of us combined. In the future, keep your fucking comments to yourself. Understood?"

Hoak snapped to attention and saluted. "Sorry, sir." She turned her attention to Alissa and Chris. "I shouldn't have been so disrespectful."

Gibson stepped over to a table and motioned for Alissa to join him. On top sat floor plans for Mass General.

"Where did you get these?"

"When the virus broke out, some of the techno guys in the government downloaded floor plans and maps of every major building and location they thought we might have to raid later for supplies and shared them with the military commands. Thank God they did, otherwise we'd be going in blind. I'd like you to brief us on everything we need to know to complete the mission."

Alissa spread out the maps in front of her and, using a stylus, spent the next fifteen minutes filling in the Marines on what had happened that day, leaving out details about the ER, the maternity ward, abandoning patients, and leaving Courtney and Stella on the roof to die. She focused primarily on Dr. Edwards and the location of the pathology lab. When finished, she turned the briefing back over to the captain.

"Okay, people. The chopper will land us on the roof. We'll make our way to the second floor by the rear stairwell, grab the blood samples, and evac out the same way we entered. It'll be a quick in and out, a snatch and grab. The potential for hostile contact is high. Plan for the best and prepare for the worst. And remember, our goal is to protect the civilian assets so they can grab the samples and we can all go home." Gibson glared at Hoak. "We leave in thirty mikes. Saddle up, people. Oorah."

The others yelled out Oorah, except for Hoak.

As the Marines prepared for combat, Gibson moved closer to Alissa and Chris, pushing the loose strand of hair back in place. "Forgive Hoak. She was with the Marine Detachment aboard the *New York*, an amphibious transport ship, when the outbreak hit. Half the crew turned. The rest had to fight their way to safety. Hoak, Foster, and Overturf were the only ones to make it off alive. They watched the Navy sink the *New York* with more than three hundred hands aboard."

Alissa nodded. She understood the private's attitude.

The five Marines assisted each other in strapping on the gear from the SITT, or Shipboard Integrated Tactical Team, the ship's SWAT team. Each wore the traditional MARSCI-RAS vest without the protective plates, leggings, arm guards, and helmets with face shields. Overturf assisted the civilians in suiting up. The Marines armed themselves with an M4 carbine, a Sig Sauer M18 9mm semi-automatic pistol with a suppressor, and a pouch containing five M67 grenades each. They each had a Ka-Bar knife strapped to their leg except for Hoak who carried World War II-era bayonets, one on each hip. Overturf brought over the same weapons for Alissa and Chris, minus the pouches of grenades.

Chris picked up the Sig Sauer and examined it. "Do these silencers work?"

"They don't eliminate the gunshot, just muffle the sound. They'll come in handy if we have to take out one or two deaders and don't want to bring the entire building down on us."

Once geared up, Gibson led the way topside to the Seahawk that had ferried Alissa and Chris to the vessel. Bellamah greeted them and helped the team aboard. As they climbed into the helicopter, Robson greeted them from the pilot's seat.

"Welcome to Robson's airborne chauffeur service."

Most of the Marines moaned, which only made him grin. Frank occupied the co-pilot's seat. Another Marine sat behind the co-pilot to provide security for the helicopter once at the hospital. He introduced himself as Private Dennis Duprau.

Bellamah climbed on last, sliding shut the troop door behind him. Robson started the engines. The rotors churned, slowly gathering speed until the familiar thump-thump-thump filled the cabin. Bellamah made his way through the cockpit, securing the team in their seats and making sure there were no live rounds in the chambers, the safeties were on, and all weapons were either holstered or pointing toward the deck. When fully warmed up, Robson lifted off the flight deck, turned west, and headed out across the harbor.

"Good morning, ladies and gentlemen. Please put your chairs and food trays in the upright position. Do not fire your weapons inside the cabin. In the event of a crash, those who survive will probably be eaten by deaders. Sit back and enjoy your flight. We know you had no choice of airlines, but we thank you for flying Miracle Air. Remember our motto…."

The Marines responded in unison. "If you get there, it's a miracle."

Alissa looked to starboard. Boston sat less than a mile away. The top ten floors of the Prudential Building had been gutted by fire and several of the glass panes of the Hancock Building had been shattered. Farther to the right stood the remnants of the Tobin Bridge, the center spans collapsed. More horrible memories rushed in, clouding her thinking. She felt her insides tighten.

Snap out of it, Alissa chastised herself. *Concentrate on the mission ahead if you want to get out of this alive.*

A few seconds later, the helicopter crossed the coast and flew over Boston.

Chapter Thirteen

THE HELICOPTER MADE landfall near Faneuil Hall Market-place at an altitude of one thousand feet. Alissa glanced out the side window. Thousands of deaders filled the streets. As one, their heads turned up and focused on the Seahawk. Some reached up. Most of them followed the helicopter inland.

"That's not good," Alissa spoke into her microphone. "We're going to attract them all to the hospital."

"Don't worry, ma'am," said Robson. "We have that covered."

As if on cue, every siren on the *Iwo Jima* went off at once. Alissa could hear the electronic wail inside the cabin even with her helmet on. Outside, the noise could be heard for miles. For the thousands of deaders roaming the streets of Boston, it was a call to dinner. The living dead turned their attention from the helicopter and wandered toward shore, hoping the sound meant food. None of them paid any attention to the humans flying overhead.

A minute later, Robson announced, "Mass General is dead ahead. There is no, repeat, no activity visible on the roof."

"Excellent," responded Gibson. "You have permission to set down."

"Roger that."

Robson maneuvered the Seahawk over the building's roof, hovered for a few seconds, then landed. As Bellamah slid open the port troop door, the team placed goggles over their eyes. Gibson's Marines jumped out and formed a semi-circle around the hatch, their weapons raised into the high-ready position. Once certain the coast was clear, Dobyns waved for the civilians to follow. Duprau jumped out and rook up position to protect the Seahawk.

"Wait here until we get back," Gibson ordered Robson. "We shouldn't be long."

"I'll keep the meter running."

Gibson jumped out of the helicopter and approached Alissa. "Where to now?"

Alissa pointed to a small structure with a door in it. "Over there. That's the stairwell leading into the hospital."

"On my six, Marines."

As they neared the stairs, Alissa noticed a pair of legs extending from behind the rear wall. "Hang on a minute."

"Make it quick," ordered Gibson.

Alissa circled around behind the structure. A small body lay beneath a bathrobe, the portion covering the head stained with dried blood. To its right, Courtney, the nurse she had met on the roof during her escape, sat against the wall, her mouth agape. She clutched the Glock Alissa had given her in her right hand, the top of her head blown open. A splatter pattern of blood and brains clung to the wall. Alissa crouched and pulled back the top of the bathrobe. Stella lay beneath it, a single bullet wound in the back of her skull and her face shattered by the exiting round. Courtney had shot Stella from behind, gave the body as proper a burial as possible under the circumstances, and then took her own life. Alissa placed the bathrobe back over Stella's head and prayed for their souls.

"Did you know them?" asked Gibson from behind her.

"Briefly, yes."

"Sorry for your loss." The sympathetic tone became more demanding. "We need to keep moving."

"I understand." Alissa stood and headed for the stairs.

The Marines stacked up in front of the door to the stairwell, lined up to enter one after another. Overturf stepped forward and opened the door. A terrible stench of decay filtered through the opening but no deaders. Overturf tossed a chemlight inside to illuminate the stairwell. Hoak moved ahead and entered, swept the area with her weapon-mounted tactical light, and waved that the coast was clear. Gibson and Dobyns took the lead, followed by the civilians, with the rest of the team bringing up the rear. Hoak opened the metal gate at the top of the landing and they proceeded downstairs, quietly and slowly.

A deader in a hospital gown, the open back revealing a severely decomposed body, stood on the fourth-floor landing. It stared blankly at the wall, not noticing them. Hoak unholstered her Sig Sauer and fired a single round into the back of its skull. The front of its head exploded, covering the wall in gore. The collapsing body made more noise than the suppressed gunshot. A muffled moan came from several floors below. The team raised their weapons, but the noise stopped and no deaders attacked.

Hoak and Overturf made their way to the fourth-floor landing, stepping over the carcass. Dobyns kept her weapon trained on the stairwell so nothing could sneak up on them. Once they were stacked and ready, Overturf opened the door and tossed a chemlight into the corridor while Hoak readied herself for what might be on the other side. Nothing sauntered through. The Marines rushed into the corridor and sliced the pie, each team member sweeping their weapon across their assigned sector of the corridor to ensure there were no threats. Once clear, the civilians were ushered in.

Alissa shivered as she stepped onto the floor. Off to her left were the rooms with the patients she had abandoned on that first day. Across from her stood Jim Brody's room, whom she had overdosed with morphine to put out of his misery. Her thoughts immediately went to the potential horror that lay behind each closed door and the people left to die slow, lingering deaths. Guilt wracked her soul.

Gibson whispered, "Where now?"

Alissa pointed to her left. "That stairwell will take us to the second floor. The lab is right by the exit."

"Let's move."

Hoak led the way, with Dobyns bringing up their rear. At the end of the corridor, the team stacked up. Overturf opened the stairwell door and tossed in a chemlight. Again, no deaders. Hoak entered, scanned the landing with her weapon-mounted tactical flashlight, and waved on the others. Hoak and Overturf led the way, pausing at each landing to scout the floor below them. Dobyns brought up the rear, shoving a wooden wedge under the door leading to the third-floor corridor so nothing could sneak up behind them.

"I'm surprised the emergency lights are still working," said Gibson.

"The back-up generators run off of solar energy," explained Alissa.

"Let's be grateful for the small favors."

Two minutes later, they stood in front of the lab.

"Let's do this," ordered Gibson.

Alissa stared at the keypad on the wall. The LED glowed red. "Shit."

"What?"

"We need an ID card to get in."

"It would have been nice to know that before we arrived." Even whispered, the anger was evident in the Gibson's tone.

Alissa pointed down the corridor. "There should be one at the nurse's station."

The team made their way to the desk halfway down the hall. Gibson and Dobyns stood at one end and Hoak and Overturf the other, each guarding their end of the corridor. Foster took up a position in front of the elevator. Alissa went behind the station and rummaged through the scattered paperwork where she had found the first ID she had used. Nothing. Opening each drawer, she searched through them. Again nothing.

"Damn it," she mumbled.

Hoak sighed. "I can't believe we came all the way in here to have the civilian fuck it up."

Gibson's tone echoed the private's frustration. "Ma'am, we have other ways of getting into the lab."

"I got this," Alissa replied nervously, ignoring what the captain had said. "Nurses are always leaving their badges behind."

Overturf rolled his eyes.

"Is there anywhere else you can look?" asked Chris.

"Let me check the break room."

Gibson snapped his fingers. "Hoak, Overturf. Clear the…."

Alissa did not wait for the Marines. She went over to the door behind the desk and entered without knocking.

"Dammit!" The captain motioned to Overturf and Hoak. "Stop her from getting herself killed."

A nurse sat at the table with a huge chunk of flesh ripped out of her shoulder, dried blood staining the front and back of her scrubs. Alissa gasped, only then realizing that it was not one of the living dead. A scalpel with encrusted blood sat on the table. A long, deep cut ran down the length of her arm from the wrist to the elbow, severing the artery. She must have been bitten and decided to take her own life rather than turn. Alissa did not blame her.

"Poor woman," said Chris.

"There's one good thing about her taking her life."

"What's that?"

Alissa pointed to the corpse. The nurse's ID card hung from a lanyard around her neck. Alissa entered the room, clasped both sides of the lanyard, and began lifting it off the woman's neck.

As she did, the nurse opened its eyes and lunged at Alissa.

Chapter Fourteen

A LISSA RELEASED THE lanyard and jumped back, barely missing being bit in the arm. Overturf entered the break room, raised his carbine, and fired five rounds into its head and chest, blasting it across the break room. It slid down the wall and slumped forward, its shattered ribcage allowing its lungs and heart to slide onto the floor. Alissa rushed forward, grabbed the lanyard, and yanked it from around the deader's neck. She and Chris raced out of the break room.

Out in the corridor, the Marines focused their aim on the break room. Being closest to the nurse's station, Foster stepped back when he heard the gunfire to give himself more room to respond. When he did, he inadvertently pressed the call button for the elevator. The door slid aside. Seven deaders reached out, grabbed Foster, and dragged him inside. Six bit their prey, none of them able to break through the arm pads and leggings. The last, a doctor in a blood-stained white lab coat with half its face chewed off, clutched at the private's helmet and face shield, its rotted teeth scraping against the thick plastic.

"Get these fucking things off me!"

Overturf centered himself in the door. He couldn't shoot without risking wounding his friend. He shouldered his weapon and withdrew the Ka-Bar knife strapped to his leg. The closest deader, one in a tattered EMT uniform, attempted to chew on Foster's right leg. Overturf drove the blade through the deader's skull with such force it pierced the opposite temple and sliced into Foster's leg. The private cried out from pain.

"You stabbed me, you bastard."

Spotting the new prey, and hoping for an easier meal, five of the deaders stood and stumbled out of the elevator. Overturf jumped over the nurse's station, drawing them away from his friend. Three reached across the counter toward him. The other two staggered toward Hoak. Overturf took down the three in front of him with two rounds to their heads, careful that no stray bullets passed through into the elevator.

From both ends of the corridor, deaders emerged from the rooms where they had been drawn to the noise made by the *Iwo Jima* in Boston Harbor, now attracted to the melee inside the hospital. Nine stumbled from the rooms nearest the lab and another nineteen from the rooms on the opposite end, the largest number exiting the maternity ward that had been overrun on day one.

Alissa and Chris left the break room in time to see the carnage taking place. Alissa tapped Chris on the shoulder. "Let's get those samples."

"Stay with us," ordered Hoak, but too late. The two civilians were already halfway to the lab. Hoak swore and set off after them, pushing her way to the front and taking down deaders with her carbine. Chris helped clear the way. Alissa held the ID card, ready to scan it.

THE DOCTOR DEADER attempting to rip off Foster's face shield knelt beside the Marine, its upper body above him. Foster found it difficult to move because of the knife wound in his leg, so his only defense was to push away the deader with his left hand while punching it with his right. Because of the poor leverage, Foster couldn't knock it off him. With only one option left, Foster pulled the Sig Sauer from its holster and emptied the magazine into the deader's chest. The bullets punched harmlessly into decayed flesh but the force of the shots pushed it away. The deader fell back against the elevator wall, tearing off Foster's face shield.

"CONTACT FRONT," YELLED Gibson as he made his way down the corridor.

Taking down the deaders was easy. Having been turned on the first day of the outbreak with no food since then, they were listless and uncoordinated, rendering them easy targets. Gibson went to one knee and fired into the pack as Dobyns stood behind the captain and fired over his head. The captain ran out of ammunition first and called out, "Loading." Dobyns aimed at a female deader in sweatpants and t-shirt and blasted two rounds into its head. Dobyns had killed so many deaders since the outbreak began that it had become second nature to her, to the point she saw this as an act of kindness rather than slaughter.

Gibson finished reloading. "Where the hell is rest of the team?"

"Overturf is helping Foster. Hoak is chasing after the civilians."

"Fuck."

The two eventually cleared the corridor. However, nothing could prepare them for the last two deaders that emerged from the maternity ward.

One was a nurse, its scrubs torn open and the flesh and muscles eaten down to the exposed ribs. In its right hand, it clutched the leg of a newborn like a turkey leg, most of the infant having been devoured. A second deader emerged behind it wearing a soiled hospital gown. An umbilical cord extended from under the gown. As it entered the corridor, Dobyns noticed a dead baby attached to the other end, being dragged behind what once was its mother. She froze, unable to fire on these two.

Gibson stepped in front of her and took down the last two deaders, then fired two rounds into each infant. Dobyns bent over, lifted her face shield, and puked on the floor. As she spit out the last of the vomitus, Gibson moved alongside her.

"Hold it together, Marine. You can't fold on me now."

"I won't, sir."

FOSTER AIMED HIS M4 at the doctor deader, centering on its head, and pulled the trigger. One round fired before the bolt stuck open. The bullet blasted off its left temple but missed the limbic system. Grabbing the handrail, Foster pulled himself into a standing position and limped toward the exit as the elevator door closed. He punched the open button.

Before the door could open again, the deader climbed to its feet and attacked, its teeth sinking into his left ear and ripping it off. Foster cried out and shoved it away. The deader opened its mouth, letting the morsel fall out, and lunged again.

OVERTURF RACED OVER to help his friend as the elevator closed. He frantically pressed the call button several times. When the doors opened, he stepped back and raised his carbine. The doctor deader had wedged Foster into the corner of the elevator and was chewing on his face. The left eye, nose, and cheek had already been devoured. Overturf placed the barrel against the deader's head and fired two rounds. It dropped to the floor.

Foster raised his hands to his face, felt the torn flesh and bone beneath, then pulled them away and stared at the blood.

"I'm so sorry, man." Overturf reached out to comfort his friend.

Foster brushed his arm away. "Kill me."

"I can't do that."

"If you don't, I'll become one of them." Fear welled in Foster's eyes. "Please."

Overturf aimed the carbine at his friend. Foster closed his

eyes and muttered his final words.

"Thank you."

Overturf fired a single round into Foster's forehead.

HOAK RAN OUT of ammunition before she reached the last deader dressed in a Boston Police uniform. She slung the M4 over her shoulder and withdrew the twin bayonets from their scabbards. She plunged the first up through the deader's jaw, the blade slicing through the roof of its mouth and imbedding in the frontal lobe. It tried to snarl, its efforts hampered by the bladed weapon. Hoak plunged the second bayonet into the deader's neck where the spine and skull met. It froze when the blade pierced its limbic system. She twisted the bayonet until the deader went limp and dropped to the floor, yanking the weapons from her hands.

"Open that fucking door," Hoak yelled.

Alissa was already on it. When the red light on the keypad flashed green, she shoved open the door. The corpse of Doctor Edwards sat where she had left him.

Alissa rushed inside. "We're clear."

Chris followed, stopping in the doorway to check on Hoak.

The private had wasted precious seconds trying to pull her bayonets from the police deader's corpse. She had not noticed the pair from the elevator shambling toward her.

"Hoak," called out Chris. "Behind you."

The private glanced over her shoulder as the two deaders attacked. Chris aimed his carbine at the same moment Hoak stood, blocking his view. One deader grabbed each arm. Hoak ran for the door, dragging them behind her. Chris swung his weapon around to smash the stock into their faces. As Hoak entered the doorway, one of the deaders bit down on her shoulder, its teeth plunging through her uniform and sinking into her flesh. She felt a sharp pain from the bite and blood running down her skin.

Chris went to help her.

"Forget about me. I'm already dead. Get those fucking blood samples."

Chris knew what he had to do. So did Hoak. Reaching out, he slipped his hand into the pouch containing the grenades and removed one. She nodded her approval. Chris yanked the pin, dropped the grenade back into the pouch, and, placing his right foot on Hoak's chest, pushed her and the deaders down the corridor. Ducking back inside, he slammed the door and dropped prone.

The grenades exploded, tearing apart Hoak and her attackers. Shrapnel tore through the door to the lab and warped the jamb. It also ripped through the corridor walls, shattering the oxygen and gas lines behind its surface, which ignited. The secondary blast collapsed the ceiling, which cascaded into the corridor, burying the carcasses.

Chapter Fifteen

THE DEADERS SURROUNDING Hoak absorbed most of the blast from the grenades, sparing Gibson, Overturf, and Dobyns from shrapnel. Even so, their training told them to duck and turn from the blast to protect their faces. A loud crumbling sound followed the explosions. Dobyns glanced over her shoulder in time to see the roof collapse.

"What the fuck happened?" asked Overturf.

"Looks like Hoak set off her grenades."

"What about the civilians?" Gibson stood and shook the dust from his shoulders.

"I can't see them."

"Fuck." Gibson rushed past the others toward the debris, afraid of what he might find. He recognized Hoak only by the tattered limbs in military fatigues that had been ripped from her body in the blast. Nothing else was left. Two other bodies lay beside Hoak's remains. Neither wore the clothes the civilians had.

"Alissa, Chris. Are you okay?"

No answer.

Gibson started to climb over the debris when a snarl came from above him. A deader in a Boston College sweatshirt stumbled off the edge of the floor where the blast had torn open the ceiling. He jumped back a moment before the deader fell onto the spot where he had stood. The captain shot it in the back of the head as two more fell through the opening. The ceiling above him groaned. Gibson retreated as a ten-foot section collapsed into the corridor, adding to the pile of debris and dropping another seven deaders onto their floor.

Overturf raised his carbine but Gibson lowered the barrel. "Don't waste your ammunition. We'll go up to the fourth floor and come down the other stairwell."

"What if the civilians are dead?" asked Dobyns.

"It doesn't matter. We know where the blood samples are and we still need to get them. Move out."

Gibson set off for the other end of the hospital with the remnants of his team.

"WHAT WAS THAT?" asked Duprau, who stood outside the Seahawk.

"Sorry?" asked Robson.

"That rumble. Didn't you feel it? I think it was an explosion."

"I didn't feel anything."

A second, larger explosion rumbled from deep inside the hospital.

Duprau snapped the pilot an I-told-you-so glance. Robson spoke into the microphone. "Retrieval Team, this is Sky King. Do you copy? Over."

No response.

"Retrieval Team, this is Sky King. Do you copy? Over."

Still no response.

"Damn it, answer me."

Silence.

"Fuck!"

"Should I check on them?" asked Duprau.

"You can't leave the helicopter. We don't have a large enough security team as it is. What if they return with a pack of deaders on their ass?"

"What if they need our help?" asked Frank.

"I know." Robson contemplated his options, which were limited. "Check along the sides of the building for any signs of them or where that explosion occurred. Stay on the roof and be ready to haul ass back here if I call you."

"Roger that."

Duprau made his way to the southern portion of the roof.

GIBSON REACHED THE other end of the corridor and paused for Overturf and Dobyns to raise their weapons. When they were stacked, he cracked open the stairwell door a few inches and tossed a chemlight through the opening. He half expected to be swarmed by deaders. The stairs were empty. The noise of hundreds of the living dead on every floor, agitated by the gunfire and explosion, echoed off the walls. Thank God none of them made it in here or this whole mission would be over.

Motioning for the others to follow, Gibson entered the stairwell and ascended, with Overturf following and Dobyns bringing up the rear, closing and sticking wooden wedges under the doors to ensure no deaders snuck up on them from behind. The captain paused on the third floor to look through the window. Every deader on that floor staggered toward the spot where the floor had caved in, disappearing one by one through the hole.

"What do you see?" asked Overturf.

"Check it out." Gibson stepped aside so the corporal could have a turn.

"Shit."

"Let me see," said Dobyns. Overturf stepped aside for her.

Dobyns shook her head. "We're going to have a Charlie Foxtrot waiting for us when we get back to the second floor."

"We'll worry about that later. Keep moving."

Gibson led the way to the fourth floor. As they approached the landing, he spotted a deader in a sanitation worker's uniform bumping against the door trying to get through. The captain pulled his Ka-Bar knife from its scabbard.

"I got this."

Gibson quietly made his way to the landing and crept up behind the deader. When within two feet, he whistled. The deader stumbled around. The moment it faced him, Gibson drove the blade through its right eye and down toward the base of the spine, waiting until the hilt struck bone before twirling it around, scrambling the deader's limbic system. He grabbed it by the collar and gently lowered the body to the floor, then withdrew the knife and wiped the blade on its uniform. As Overturf pulled the corpse to one side, Gibson peered through the window.

"Fuck!"

"What's wrong?" asked Overturf.

"See for yourself." Gibson stepped aside for the corporal.

Close to fifty deaders packed the other end of the corridor, scratching at the stairwell door trying to get down to the noise. "Where did they come from?"

"They must have been in the rooms when we passed through the corridor earlier."

Dobyns pushed her way through to have a look. "You've got to be fucking kidding. How are we going to fight our way through that?"

"We've already used half our ammo," Gibson answered. "If we clear this corridor, we run the risk of going Winchester."

"We have no choice," said Dobyns.

"Maybe we do, sir." Overturf pointed to the rooms on the left. "On the ride in, I saw scaffolding covering that side of the building. I could lure those things into one of the rooms and escape via the outside. While they're distracted, you and Dobyns can sneak by. I'll make my way to the roof and rejoin you in a few minutes."

"That's crazy," snorted Dobyns.

"Crazy enough it might work." Gibson thought about the

plan for a moment. "Go ahead and give it a try. If things go south, we'll move in and bail you out. And no fucking heroics. I don't want to lose any more people today."

"Trust me, I want to get home, too."

Gibson quietly opened the door and Overturf slipped through, proceeding cautiously so as not to make any noise. The captain gently closed the door behind him.

OVERTURF MADE IT halfway down the corridor without being detected. He paused by the room before the stairwell leading to the roof and peered inside, making certain no deaders were hidden there. Once certain of his escape route, he raised his carbine and emptied an entire magazine into the last row of deaders. Several heads exploded, the lifeless bodies dropping to the floor. As he switched out magazines, the rest of the horde turned in his direction.

"Come on, motherfuckers. Get yourself a nice hot meal."

The deaders shambled down the corridor.

Overturf ducked into the room, raced over to the window, and fired five rounds from his Sig Sauer into the glass, shattering it. Using the stock of the carbine to clear away the shards, he crawled through onto the scaffolding and waited. A minute later, the first of the deaders entered the room, followed by the others. The deaders stopped, uncertain where their meal had gone. Overturf whistled. On seeing him crouching outside the window, the pack rushed forward. The corporal fired into the approaching horde, taking down another seven. When they reached the window, Overturf stood and moved aside a few feet.

As he switched out magazines, a deader in a nurse's uniform, its blonde hair disheveled and half its face eaten away, stuck its head through the pane. Reaching out, it grabbed Overturf by the leg. He jumped back. It maintained its hold, knocking him off balance. Overturf landed on his back on the planks, knocking the air out of him. The full magazine dropped out of his hand and plummeted off the scaffolding. The nurse deader pulled itself through the window and dragged itself up his leg. Overturf kicked it in the face, with no effect. He continued pummeling the nurse deader with his boot until its skull fractured and its lower jaw dislodged. The deader loosened its grip enough so Overturf could break free. He rolled onto his stomach, scrambled to his feet, and retreated several feet down the planks.

By now, half a dozen deaders had crawled out onto the scaffolding and lumbered toward him, the nurse in the lead. Overturf unholstered his Sig Sauer fired a round that caught it in the gaping mouth, blowing out the back of its head. The body tumbled to one side, falling off the planks and getting caught up in the diagonal brace, dangling off the side. The others pushed past and surged toward Overturf as even more of the living dead made their way onto the scaffolding.

Overturf spun around and ran to the far end, looking for a way to escape.

DUPRAU HAD FINISHED checking the east side of the building for any signs of the explosion when he heard gunshots outside coming from the north. Rushing over to that side of the roof, he leaned over the ledge in time to see Overturf on the scaffolding backing away from a horde of deaders.

"Hey."

Overturf looked around for whoever called him.

"Up here."

The corporal turned to the roof and spotted Duprau.

"Make your way to the end and climb up."

Overturf ran to the end of the scaffolding with the deaders close behind.

WHEN THE LAST of the deaders entered the room, Gibson waved for Dobyns to join him. They snuck out into the corridor and quietly made their way to the opposite side of the building. Gibson paused when he reached the room filled with the living dead, closing the door and shoving a wooden wedge under it so none of them could escape. The two Marines proceeded to the opposite end of the corridor, entered the stairwell, and made their way to the second floor.

OVERTURF REACHED THE end of the planking and crawled around to the outside of the horizontal braces which he used as a ladder. The maneuver took too long and, before he could climb more than a few feet, the deaders reached him. Five pairs of hands stretched through the scaffolding and grabbed at him, clutching his legs and pulling him against the frame. Several sets of teeth bit into his extremities, thankfully unable to break through the leggings or arm shields. Overturf kicked, trying to break free. Every time he dislodged one set of hands, another grasped on to him. Three deaders made their way around the edge of the catwalk to get at their prey. The rest surged against those pressed against the deaders holding on to the corporal, crushing their weight against the frame.

The scaffolding swayed.

"Hurry up," yelled Duprau.

"I can't." Panic filled Overturf's voice. "The bastards won't let go."

Duprau raised the carbine and aimed but could not fire without the risk of hitting Overturf. Placing the weapon on the roof, he reached over the ledge, holding onto the lip with his left hand and extending his right. "I'll pull you up."

Overturf reached up and clutched onto Duprau.

At that moment, the combined weight of the deaders over-whelmed the scaffolding. With a horrifying groan of metal, the structure's support beams bent and tilted away from the building. Rather than release the Marine, Overturf clasped his hand tighter, hoping it would save him. It condemned them both. As the scaffolding toppled to one side, Overturf pulled Duprau off the roof. The metal structure, the two men, and over forty deaders crashed into the parking lot below. Fortunately for Overturf, he died on impact, his head cracking open on the pavement and the contents of his abdomen bursting through his uniform. Duprau shattered his spine, broke his leg, and ruptured several internal organs, leaving him paralyzed and in agonizing pain.

Over half the deaders died in the fall, either being crushed by the metal or having their heads smashed open upon hitting the pavement. Those not killed went after the food they had fought so hard to obtain. A dozen crawled over to Overturf, a couple feasting on his face, the others ripping into the organs that had burst through his skin. Duprau was not as lucky. With no way to fight back, he could only scream in agony as seven of the living dead descended upon him and fed. Three tore open his chest, pulled out his intestines, and gorged. One chewed on his neck and the others fed around the compound fracture of his broken right leg. Duprau's last conscious moment was when two deaders tore off his right arm and fought over the morsel like cats battling over a mouse. Thankfully, at that point he passed out from pain.

ROBSON HAD BEEN keeping an eye on Duprau from the helicopter to make sure nothing snuck up behind him. He watched in confusion as the Marine aimed the M4 over the side of the building and then leaned over the ledge. Shock replaced confusion when he watched the man yanked off the roof.

"Stay here," he ordered Frank and Bellemah. Jumping out of the helicopter, Robson ran over to the ledge and peered over the side.

From the carnage in the parking lot below, he surmised that Duprau must have been trying to help one of the Marines to escape when the scaffolding collapsed. Picking up the carbine, he aimed at the Marine's head and fired several rounds until his skull exploded then did the same for Duprau. The rest of the magazine he emptied into the deaders, butchering as many as he could until the ammunition ran out.

Racing back to the helicopter, he climbed into his seat and put on his helmet.

"What's going on?" asked Frank.

"A fucking shit show." He held the microphone to his lips. "Retrieval Team, this is Sky King. Do you copy? Over."

No answer. Damn it. The situation inside the building must be going south.

"Can anybody hear me? If so, please respond."

Still nothing.

Focusing his attention on the door leading into the hospital, Robson prayed the rest of the team would come through soon.

GIBSON GLANCED THROUGH the window of the stairwell door. More deaders had fallen through from the third floor. A pack swarmed between them and the door to the lab.

"What are we going to do now?" whispered Dobyns.

"I'm thinking."

Chapter Sixteen

SHRAPNEL FROM HOAK'S grenades had pierced the walls and door of the lab but had missed Chris, who had fallen prone. Alissa had ducked when Chris did, sparing her from being wounded, though a few shards had whizzed past her head. Once things died down, she ran over to Chris.

"What the fuck did you do?"

"I'm fine, thanks." He groaned and slowly rose to his feet, steadying himself on a nearby lab table.

Alissa punched him in the chest, making no effort to contain her anger. "You killed Hoak."

"She'd been bitten."

"Did you have to use grenades?"

"Hoak told me to."

Alissa huffed.

"You're welcome for saving your life. *Again.*"

Alissa stepped back and shook her head. "You're fucking insane."

"Just get what we came for." Chris leaned against the lab table.

When Alissa turned around, she noticed Dr. Edwards seated in the chair where she had left him. The body had decomposed over the months, most of the flesh and tissue having rotted away. She could still detect the gaping wound in his right abdomen from where the deader had bitten him. The intestines he had held in now lay on the floor, shriveled and decayed. A pool of bodily fluids had formed beneath the seat and flies and maggots swarmed over the body. Only then did she become aware of the horrible stench.

"Hurry up," ordered Chris. "Before I puke."

Alissa ignored him and crossed over to the refrigerator on the far wall. Opening the door, she was relieved to find that the unit still worked. Thank God for solar-run emergency power. She retrieved the two vials of the doctor's blood. Thinking for a moment, she opened the doors to the wall shelves and rummaged through them.

"What are you doing?"

"Looking for something to protect them. If these get broken, everything we've gone through is for nothing."

On the fifth try, she found a stack of gauze pads. Removing three, she wrapped one around each of the vials and the third around them both. She slipped the wad into the inside pocket of her leather jacket and zipped up the front. As she passed by Edwards, she used two fingers to gently close his eyelids. Fluid flowed from the beneath them.

"What you did won't be in vain," she whispered to the corpse.

"Are you ready?" snapped Chris.

"I am." Alissa approached the door and paused. "But we're not going anywhere."

"What do you mean?"

She pointed to the monitor above the door attached to the camera outside. Cracks distorted the lens from the explosion.

Chris stepped back and mumbled, "Fuck."

A pack of deaders milled around the door. He counted eight but knew there were probably more not visible.

"We'll fight our way out."

"We'll never get through that," said Alissa.

Chris flashed her a contemptuous glare. "We've made it through worse. I'll hold them off while you make a break for the stairwell and head to the roof. I'll be right behind you."

"You'll be killed."

"No, I won't. I'm insane, remember?" Chris raised his carbine. "When I tell you to, open the door and be prepared to run."

"Please, be careful." Alissa grabbed the knob and waited.

Chris took a deep breath and prepared to kill off the pack on the other side. "Now."

Alissa turned the knob and pulled. The door didn't open. She tried again, the noise attracting the attention of the deaders outside which swarmed the lab.

"What's wrong?" asked Chris.

Alissa moved back. "The explosion warped the jamb."

"Shit!"

"Great move with the grenades."

"Get off my back. I saved your ass out there."

"And you trapped us in here because you had to fucking show off again."

"Screw you." Chris moved in front of Alissa, pointing a finger in her face. "The only reason we're here is because of Nathan."

"We're here to get the vaccine to save the world." Each word out of Alissa's mouth seethed with anger.

"The only reason the military knows about those blood samples is because you had to get Nathan to their clinic to save his life, and almost got us killed in the process. And you know damn well you're hoping these samples might save his life. This is all about you."

"That's not true."

"It is, you just refuse to admit it."

"Then why did you come along?"

Chris stared at her, incredulous. "Because for some reason I care about you. It's why I saved Archer and why I came along on this suicide mission. Not that it matters. You only give a shit about that damned cat and your precious Nathan."

Alissa slapped Chris across the face. His expression changed, more hurt than angry. Before he could respond, she reached out again, this time cupping his head in her hands. Their lips touched as she kissed him deeply and lustfully. She pulled him close. Despite them being moments from death, she felt him against her growing erect inside his pants. Despite his arousal, he gently pushed her away.

"What are you doing?"

"Stop asking questions." Alissa turned around, slid her pants and panties down around her knees, and sat on the lab table. "If we're going to die, I want you to know how much I care about you."

Chris stepped up to Alissa and unzipped himself, freeing his erection. He paused.

"What are you waiting for?" Alissa's tone had more desire in it than frustration.

Grabbing Alissa by the hips, Chris entered her, eliciting a moan of pleasure. For the next few minutes, they vented their anger, frustrations, and concern for each other in rough sex, oblivious to the horde of deaders scratching at the door trying to get at them.

Chapter Seventeen

S PARKS SAT BESIDE the radio, his feet on the console and the headset around his neck, impatiently waiting for word from the recovery team in Boston. They had lifted off from the *Iwo Jima* more than an hour ago. Not that he expected the retrieval to be quick, but Sparks could not shake that gut feeling that the situation had gone bad.

He nearly jumped out of his chair when West opened the door to the radio room and barged in.

Sparks removed the headset from around his neck. "You scared the shit out of me, sir."

"Sorry. Any word from the recovery team?"

"Not yet. But it's only been a little over an hour."

"Try to reach them. There's been a change of plans?"

Sparks' gut feeling grew more intense. "How so?"

"A nor'easter is bearing down on us fast. It's already snowing outside. Our meteorologist says this will be a big one. If they fly back to the *Iwo Jima* it could be a couple of days before we can land them here. Carrington and Anderson want Robson to fly back to Warren Island directly from Boston."

"Roger that."

"Thanks." West headed for the door and paused. "Let me know when you get a confirmation from the team."

"I will, sir."

Sparks placed the headset over his ears and made the call. "Sky King, this is Alpha Base. Do you copy? Over."

Robson's voice came over the radio. It sounded stressed.

"Sparks, is that you?"

"Who else would it be? How's the retrieval going?"

"It's gone into full FUBAR mode."

The gut feeling became a knot in the pit of Spark's stomach. "How so?"

"We heard an explosion inside the hospital a few minutes ago. I lost a Marine when he went to save a member of the retrieval team trying to escape a pack of deaders."

"What about the rest of the team?"

"I've had no radio contact with them since they entered the hospital. I don't know if there's a problem with their comms or if they're all dead."

"Shit." Sparks tried not to let the information rattle him. "I need to inform you about a change in plans. There's a huge nor'easter heading our way."

"That fucking figures."

"The eggheads here want those blood samples as soon as possible. When you take off, head straight back to base and not to the *Iwo Jima*. Do you copy?"

"I copy."

"Let me know when you lift off and I'll guide you in."

"Thanks. Jesus, can this day get any worse? Over and out."

Sparks didn't bother responding. He knew the answer to that question.

KIERA STOOD BY the window of Nathan's hospital room, watching the first flakes of snow cover the grass and trees. She had not spoken or moved from this spot in an hour. Shithead curled up at her feet. Rebecca sat in the recliner by the bed, her attention shifting from Nathan tied securely to the frame, the magazine she absent-mindedly thumbed through, and the weather outside.

"Isn't the snow beautiful?" asked Rebecca, hoping to engage the teenager.

"It'd be a lot more beautiful if Alissa and Chris were back." Kiera turned from the window. "What's taking them so long?"

"They've only been gone a few hours. They're not expected back until later today, or maybe tomorrow if this storm gets any worse."

"Damn."

"Relax."

"How can I relax? God only knows what's happening to them."

"I'm sure they'll be fine," comforted Rebecca. "Alissa and Chris know how to take care of themselves. Besides, they have Marines with them. Don't worry until you hear bad—"

The door to the hospital room opened. Both women glanced over, relieved to see a nurse enter. She stopped on spotting Kiera and Rebecca.

"I'm sorry to bother you. I'm Elaine. I'm here to check the patient's vital signs and take some blood."

"Go ahead," said Kiera. "You're not bothering us."

"Do you need me to move?" asked Rebecca.

"No. You're fine."

Elaine went over to the opposite side of the hospital bed and checked the heart monitor and IV drip, then took Nathan's blood pressure.

"How is he?" asked Rebecca.

"Stable."

"Do you think that means the blood they're retrieving from Boston might reverse the virus?"

"You'd have to ask the doctors about that." Elaine removed a hypodermic needle and two empty vials from her pocket. "They should be by to check on your friend in a few hours. I'll be at the nursing station until six. If you want to go get something to eat at the mess hall, I'll keep an eye on him."

"We'll think about it."

Elaine tapped Nathan's arm, searching for a good spot.

Finding a large vein, she slid the needle under the skin and inserted the first vial. When she pushed it down, blood filled the glass chamber.

"Any word on the team that went to Boston?" asked Kiera.

Elaine shook her head and switched out vials. "I'm a nurse. They don't tell us stuff like that. If I hear anything, I'll let you know."

Shithead stood up and walked around the side of the bed to Elaine, curious to see what went on. She did not notice him. She filled and removed the second vial, then prepared a piece of gauze and attached it to tape to cover the wound. As she removed the hypodermic, Shithead placed his front paws on the bed and lifted himself up, startling Elaine. She jumped, accidentally jabbing herself with the needle.

"Damn it!"

Rebecca stood. "What happened?"

"That God damn dog scared me."

Kiera called Shithead, who bowed his head and made his way over to her.

Elaine disposed of the needle, placed the bandage on Nathan's puncture, and stepped over to the sink. Removing her latex gloves, Elaine massaged the area around the needle-stick, encouraging the wound to bleed. After a few seconds of pushing, a tiny drop of blood formed on the tip of her finger. She placed her finger under cold running water and cleaned it with soap.

"Are you okay?" asked Kiera.

"I stuck myself with that needle. There's not much blood." Elaine attempted to maintain a calm demeanor. "I'll be fine."

"Are you sure? Is there anything we can do?"

Elaine shook her head and picked up the two vials. "I'll have Carrington check it out to be on the safe side. In the meantime, I'll have another nurse take over. Call her if you need anything. She'll be down the hall."

After Elaine left, Kiera gently slapped Shithead in the butt.

"Bad dog."

He whimpered, but his tail wagged as soon as she petted him.

Rebecca sat down. "Why don't you take Shithead for a walk and get dinner. I'll stay with Nathan."

"I'm fine."

"No, you need something to eat." When Kiera started to protest, Rebecca cut her off. "Besides, I need you to bring me back something."

"I suppose there's no use in arguing?"

Rebecca flashed her a look of disapproval.

"Fine." Kiera headed for the door. "Come on, Shithead. Time to eat."

The dog barked his approval and followed Kiera out of the room.

MIRIAM, STEVE, AND the children spent the morning and first half of the afternoon cleaning the rest of the cabin. For Steve and the kids, it was an unpleasant task that had to be done, and the sooner the better. For Miriam, work provided a distraction from her thoughts. It had succeeded for a while, focusing her mind away from the threat the group faced from deaders, how close they had all come to be killed, and how tenuous their situation remained.

A little after two o'clock, when Miriam and the kids had finished cleaning everything inside except for Alissa's room, she told the kids to take a break while she prepared lunch. That's when her mind went into overdrive. It gnawed at her that they had not heard from Alissa and the others. The trip to Warren Island should have lasted eight hours at most, yet they had been gone for over thirty without a word. The more time that passed, the greater became Miriam's concern. No, that was too mild. Anxiety better described it. Anxiety over not knowing what had happened to Alissa and Chris. Anxiety over whether Nathan had recovered from his wound or had reanimated and attacked the others. Anxiety over agreeing to allow Kiera to go with them. She never should have given in. If Kiera didn't come back, it would be her fault.

Miriam chastised herself for thinking that way. Anything that happened to her family or Connie was not because of her. The fault lay with the world having gone to shit and being overrun by the living dead. The two times they had come closest to being killed had been at their own home, the first in Nahant when they barely escaped the island being swarmed by deaders and then two days ago here in the cabin. As much as Miriam had tried to fight the notion for the past few months, she eventually accepted the realization that death was inescapable, at least for most of them. Nothing she could do would prevent it. No amount of protectiveness, no supposed safe haven, nothing would deter the unavoidable. The best she could hope for would be to delay their deaths and pray that the outbreak ended before all life on earth did. Sadly, even her religious faith had been strained by recent events.

Miriam tried to concentrate on making lunch – tuna fish sandwiches with carrot sticks. She had more than enough distractions from Archer who came running when he heard the can opener. As she dumped the canned meat into a bowl, she had to contend with the cat who pulled the bowl toward him, convinced it belonged to him. Three times she moved the bowl back in front of her and, each time, Archer dragged it back. Finally, she dropped several chunks of tuna in a can containing the excess juice and placed it on the floor. Archer persisted on going after the larger bounty. Miriam picked up the cat and petted him.

"Now I know why Alissa calls you Asshat."

She placed Archer by the can, the contents of which he devoured with a loud purr.

When Miriam finished mixing the tuna and preparing the

sandwiches, she brought out the four plates and placed them on the dining room table, then returned to the kitchen to retrieve four bottles of water. She called the rest of the family for lunch.

Little Stevie and Connie came from upstairs. Both seemed upset.

"What's wrong?"

"We can't find Archer anywhere," answered Connie.

"That's because he's in the kitchen mooching."

The kids sat down. Little Stevie frowned. "Tuna fish again?"

"I've been busy this afternoon."

Connie raised the sandwich to her mouth and paused. "It looks almost like new in here. You've done a good job."

"*We've* done a good job. Thank you for helping me." Miriam suppressed the thought that all the bullet holes and memories would forever tar this place for her.

"It still smells." Little Stevie raised the sandwich to his mouth then sniffed it. "Or it could be this."

"I'll open the windows later and air out the place." She leaned back and yelled upstairs. "Steve, lunch is ready."

"He's outside, Aunt Miriam. I saw him lighting the bonfire." Connie laid her sandwich on her plate. "Do you want me to get him?"

"I'll do that, thanks. Just don't let Asshat eat our sandwiches while I'm gone."

"Roger that." Connie saluted and went back to eating.

Miriam found her husband standing by the funeral pyre tending to the flames. The air stunk of burned flesh. She walked up and hugged him from behind. "Lunch is ready."

Steve clasped her hands and squeezed. "I'll be in once the fire is out."

"I thought you were going to do this tonight so no one would see the smoke."

"I want to get it done before the snow hit."

"What makes you think it's going to snow?"

"Look at the clouds." Steve motioned toward the sky with his head. "Those are storm clouds moving in. And the temperature is in the twenties. I think we're in for a blizzard."

"Great."

"Actually, that's good. It'll put out the embers and cover the bodies in the woods so they don't decay as fast."

"I meant it'll be that much longer before Kiera and the others get back." Miriam hugged Steve tighter. "Have you tried reaching Warren Island again?"

"Three times last night and twice this morning. I'll try again after lunch." Steve broke the hug, turned around, and held Miriam close. "Don't worry. I'm sure everything is fine. Our radio is probably being affected by the storm coming in. Stop worrying."

"That's easier said than done."

"I know. But remember, no news is good news."

"You're right," said Miriam, although she didn't agree. "I'll bring our sandwiches outside and we can eat together."

"I'd like that." Steve kissed her gently. "What did you make?"

"Tuna fish."

"Oh." Steve showed about as much enthusiasm for the meal as did his son.

Miriam gently punched him in the chest. "Tell you what, I'll make hot coffee to go with it."

"Deal."

Miriam went back inside to brew a pot, still having that nagging feeling that things were about to go to shit.

Chapter Eighteen

GIBSON STARED THROUGH the small window at the deaders scratching at the door to the lab.

"I'll head up to the third floor and toss three grenades through the opening. Once the third goes off, head for the lab and retrieve the blood samples. You should have no problems. I'll rejoin you in a minute and cover your retreat."

"How am I going to get into the lab?" asked Dobyns.

Gibson removed from his jacket pocket a small item wrapped in cloth and handed it to Dobyns. She unwrapped it.

"C4?"

"You've been trained in its use, correct?"

"Yes, sir."

"Then use just enough to blow off the handle and lock."

Dobyns smirked. "You didn't trust the civilians either?"

"I did. I just live by the code of improvise, adapt, overcome." Gibson headed up the stairs. "Good luck."

Dobyns descended a few steps toward the first floor and crouched to be out of line of any shrapnel.

CHRIS WATCHED AS Alissa pulled up her leather pants. He experienced a jumble of emotions – happiness, affection, confusion.

"What was that about?"

"We fooled around." Alissa zipped her pants and straightened her shirt and jacket.

"I know that. I didn't think you liked me in that way. You're always chewing me out."

"Because you're a loose cannon and sometimes are as a big a threat as the deaders. That doesn't mean I don't like you."

Chris smiled. "So, I'm your bad boy?"

"Think of it more like we'll probably die soon and I didn't want to go out without letting you know I cared." Alissa moved closer and kissed Chris. "Now let's figure a way to get out of here."

GIBSON REACHED THE third floor, removed the wooden wedge from under the door, and checked out the corridor. Two deaders sauntered on this side of the collapsed floor, their back to him. Five others did the same on the other end. This would be easy.

Shouldering his carbine, he removed his Sig Sauer from its holster, opened the door, and stepped into the corridor. The closest deader, a female naked except for the remains of a tattered hospital gown, its right arm chewed down to the bone, spun around to face him. It snarled. Gibson fired into its open mouth. The round destroyed its limbic system and shattered the spine. The deader's head lolled to one side before the body collapsed.

The second deader, wearing a Massachusetts State Police uniform, turned to him. Most of its face had been eaten away. Gibson switched aim and fired, hitting it square in the fore-head. The deader stumbled toward him, lost its balance, and fell past him onto the floor.

Farther down the corridor, the other five deaders turned toward the noise and moved toward him. Gibson would deal with those later. He holstered his sidearm and removed three grenades, saving the last two in case he needed them later. One by one, he pulled the pin and tossed the grenades through the opening onto the second floor, then crouched in the corner, waiting for the explosions.

THE THREE GRENADES went off at two second intervals. The first explosion tore into the outer ring of deaders surrounding the door, crippling them or ripping off arms and legs. As the first batch collapsed, the second grenade sent fragments into their heads, shattering the limbic systems, and took down the second row. The last grenade killed off half the deaders on the floor and brought down two of the three clawing at the door to the lab.

When the last grenade exploded, Dobyns jumped up, rushed to the door, and entered the corridor. She fired three rounds from her M4 into the head of the last remaining deader, blasting away its head, then shot a single round into every deader lying on the floor. With the immediate threat neutralized, she stuck the wad of C4 against the knob of the lab door.

ALISSA AND CHRIS involuntarily ducked when the grenades exploded in the corridor.

"What was that?" asked Alissa as she stood.

"Looks like the Marines are here."

Gunfire erupted in the corridor, stopping after a few seconds. Alissa ran to the door and banged on its surface. "Who's there?"

"Alissa, is that you?" Dobyns asked from the other side.

"Yes."

"We thought you were dead."

"No, Chris and I are alive. We have the blood samples but can't get out. The door is jammed from when he set off the grenades."

Chris frowned. "Really?"

"Don't worry. I'm using C4 to get you out. Find a place to take cover."

Chris led Alissa to the other end of the lab where they took shelter behind the table in the center of the room.

In the corridor, Dobyns placed additional C4 on the hinges. She set each timer for ten seconds and ducked back into the stairwell.

The C4 detonated, blowing off the knob and hinges. Chris ran over and pushed the door, which collapsed onto the pile of corpses outside. Alissa joined him. Together they climbed through into the corridor. Dobyns met them on the other side.

"Are you okay?" she asked.

"Yes."

"Where are the blood samples?"

Alissa tapped her jacket. "Right here."

"Good. Let's get out of here."

The three of them darted into the stairwell and headed to the fourth floor.

WHEN THE LAST grenade went off, Gibson stood to confront the five deaders approaching the collapsed floor. Taking them down was easy. Reholstering his Sig Sauer and unslinging his M4, he fired two shots into each head, which did the trick.

As the last one fell, an explosion shook the floor beneath him. He listened and overheard Alissa and Dobyns talking. The former said she had the blood samples. Good. All they needed to do now was escape.

Gibson spun around and faced the deader in the Massachusetts State Police uniform. The round he had placed in its forehead had failed to destroy its limbic system. It had risen to its feet and snuck up behind him, too close for the captain to use the carbine. The deader lunged, knocking the weapon out of his hands and pinning the captain against the wall. Its teeth gnashed against the plastic covering of his face shield. Gibson grabbed its collar in his left hand and pushed, keeping the thing away from him. With his right, he unholstered his Sig Sauer and placed the barrel against the deader's temple.

Seeing an opportunity, the State Trooper shifted its head to the left and sunk it teeth into Gibson's wrist. Gibson pulled the trigger, the bullet imbedding itself harmlessly into the wall. The deader tore a chunk out of the captain's wrist and chewed. As Gibson dropped the Sig Sauer, clutching his wound, the deader stepped back to savor its meal.

Gibson fell to his knees. Fear and anger took control. He knew he had moments before he turned and refused to be reanimated as one of the living dead. He leaned forward and reached for the pistol with his left hand, determined to take his own life. Using his right hand, Gibson lifted the face shield, wincing from the pain. With his left, he placed the Sig Sauer in his mouth. At that moment, the deader attacked again. It grabbed the edge of Gibson's face shield and yanked the helmet off his head. Gibson let go of the Sig Sauer as the deader sunk its decayed teeth into his neck and chomped, severing the carotid artery. As it feasted on human flesh, Gibson searched for the gun but could not find it. His body grew weak from lack of blood. Leaning against the wall, Gibson bled out.

A LIGHT DUSTING of snow drifted from the sky, speckling the hospital roof in white. *Fucking fantastic,* Robson mumbled to himself. *That's the last thing I need right now.*

As if to compound the increasingly FUBARed situation, his radio crackled followed by the voice of the comm officer aboard the *Iwo Jima*.

"Sky King, this is Home Plate. Do you copy? Over."

"Home Plate, this is Sky King. I read you loud and clear. Over."

"Actual requests a SITREP of the retrieval operation soonest. Over."

"No clue," replied Robson, knowing this news would not go over well with the captain of the *Iwo Jima*. "Radio silence from retrieval team. Unable to reestablish contact. Sky King can verify two, I say again, two KIAs. Unknown status on remainder of team. Over."

"Shit. Hang on." Things must be tense aboard the *Iwo Jima* for the com officer to swear over an open line. A few seconds later, he resumed talking. "Actual has ordered you to abort the mission. He wants you back on board before the storm hits its peak. Over."

"Roger that. Over and out."

Robson scanned the roof, hoping to see the others exiting the stairwell, though he knew that was not about to happen. He considered shutting down the helicopter and going inside to find them until he realized how stupid a move that would be. He didn't stand a chance in there by himself and, if something happened to him and the others were still alive, then they'd be stuck here.

"What are we waiting for?" asked Frank.

Robson glanced at his watch. "I'm giving them five more minutes."

"But we have our orders."

"Screw that. What are they going to do? Court martial me in the middle of the apocalypse?"

"You're the boss."

"Come on," urged Robson, his eyes focused on the door. "Hurry up."

FOUR DEADERS ON the fourth floor of the hospital, which had not made their way into the corridor when the humans first appeared, and as such were not locked in the room when Overturf led the rest there, staggered around. Noises erupted throughout the building. They could not distinguish between gunfire and explosions. All they knew was that noise meant food. As suddenly as the commotion started it ceased. The deaders stood in the corridor, confused, uncertain what to do next.

One sound caught their attention – a rhythmic, mechanical thumping that meant food was nearby. The deader closest to the stairwell leading to the roof, a doctor who had died defending his patients, heard the noise coming from above. It stumbled onto the landing and made its way up the stairs. The others followed.

Chapter Nineteen

As they passed by the third-floor landing, Dobyns paused. "Wait a minute. I want to check on the captain."

Alissa and Chris waited for her on the stairs leading to the fourth floor.

Dobyns opened the door. She spotted the State Trooper deader standing over the lifeless body of Gibson, munching on his flesh.

"Fucking bastard!"

She fired two rounds from her M4 into its head.

The thing that was once Gibson looked up, its milky white eyes focusing on Dobyns. It snarled and launched itself off the floor at her. She hesitated for a moment before swinging the carbine in its direction. Gibson pushed the weapon aside and slammed Dobyns against the wall. She fired, the bullets flying up the stairs toward Alissa and Chris. Chris cried out as one round hit the wall and ricocheted into his right leg, passing through flesh and muscles, and exiting out the other side. He dropped onto the stairs, clutching his wounded leg.

Alissa rushed over to him. "Can you stand on it?"

Chris rose and winced from pain. "I can, but it hurts like a son of a bitch."

Alissa turned to Dobyns.

The private was pinned against the wall with Gibson gnawing at her face shield, trying to reach the flesh underneath. Dobyns maneuvered herself so Gibson's back faced the stairs and shoved. The captain toppled down the flight, clutching

Dobyns' carbine and threatening to pull her along with it. She grabbed the railings at the last second before being dragged down. Gibson came after her again, this time its left arm entangled in the weapon's sling. Dobyns slammed her left forearm against its neck and held it in place. With her right, she hit the quick release on the sling. With the weapon free, she bodychecked Gibson, sending the deader toppling down the stairs.

"Move it!"

The three of them headed to the fourth floor, Chris taking two stairs at a time on his good leg.

"WE GOT COMPANY," said Frank.

Robson turned to the stairs as the doctor deader exited through the door and lumbered toward the helicopter.

"I got this," said Bellemah. He fired a single round that caught the doctor deader in the mouth, ripping through its limbic system and splattering the wall behind it in gore and congealed blood.

Even Robson had to admit the uselessness of waiting around any longer. Time to head back to the *Iwo Jima*.

DOBYNS HEARD FOOTSTEPS behind her. She spun around as Gibson raced toward her. Raising her leg, she kicked it in the chest, sending it cartwheeling down the stairs. It crashed onto the landing and skid into the wall, stood up, and ran up the stairs. By now, Alissa and Chris had reached the fourth-floor landing. Alissa opened the door for Chris who limped through into the corridor.

"Don't wait for me," yelled Dobyns.

Alissa and Chris headed for the stairwell leading to the roof.

Dobyns reached the door and attempted to slam it behind her. Gibson stuck its hands through the opening, preventing her from closing it. It thrashed about furiously to get at her. She grabbed the handle with both hands and pulled back, using her weight to keep the deader from getting through.

Alissa centered herself in the doorway leading to the roof and waited for Chris.

"Hurry up."

"I'm going as fast as I can."

A snarl came from Alissa's left. A deader stood on the third step, blocking their path. She lifted the M4 and fired three rounds into its head. It collapsed, sliding down the stairs.

Taking Chris' arm and wrapping it around her shoulders, Alissa helped him. Two more deaders blocked their way, the nearest too close to use her carbine. It turned to her, exposing a mouth with no lower jaw, the chewed tongue hanging down toward its neck. Letting go of Chris, Alissa bent over, grabbed the deader behind the knees, and yanked. It toppled onto the steps. She kicked it in the face, fracturing the upper jaw, and moved on to the next. The second deader spun around and grabbed for her, its right hand mangled with three fingers missing. Alissa smashed the stock of her M4 into its face, knocking out several teeth. The deader stumbled backward, giving them room to slip by.

Chris paused at the doorway to the roof, leaning against the jamb and muttering one word. "Shit."

Alissa joined him. They watched the helicopter lifting off the roof.

ROBSON PULLED BACK on the controls and throttled the engine. The Seahawk lurched slightly and became airborne. He elevated to a height of fifteen feet and gave one last look to the stairwell, futilely hoping that—

Alissa and Chris stood by the door, the former waving frantically at him. Chris had blood oozing from a wound in his leg. At least they were still alive.

As Robson landed the helicopter, Bellemah slid open the port troop door. "Hurry up."

Alissa and Chris were already halfway to the Seahawk. She helped Chris inside and joined him. As Bellemah started to close the door, Alissa stopped him.

"Dobyns is behind us."

DOBYNS HELD ONTO the door to give the others as much of a head start as possible but knew she wouldn't be able to do so much longer. Gibson's feral attempts to reach Dobyns tired her out. It had already pushed the door open enough to get its left arm and shoulder through. When Dobyns realized she could hold it no longer, she shoved against the door as hard as she could, knocking Gibson off balance, then bolted for the stairwell leading to the roof. Whipping open the door, Gibson bolted after her. It had almost caught up to Dobyns when she turned into the stairwell, nearly tripping over the deader corpse on the landing. She jumped over it, landed on the third step, and ran up. Gibson stumbled over the body, slamming face first onto the stairs, shattering a dozen teeth and breaking its nose. Oblivious to the pain, it jumped back to its feet and pursued its prey.

A deader with no lower jaw blocked Dobyns' path. Without teeth, it posed no serious threat. She bodychecked it out of the way. The deader with the mangled right hand moved toward her. Dobyns ducked as it lunged, placing her right hand on its shoulder and pushing it down the stairs into Gibson's path. As she climbed the last few steps, the private pulled a grenade from its pouch, pulled the pin, and tossed it behind her. Rushing through the door onto the roof, Dobyns pressed her back against the wall and turned her head away from the blast. The explosion rocked the stairwell. A cloud of dust and a severed hand flew through the opening.

Ahead of Dobyns, the helicopter hovered two feet above the roof. Bellemah crouched by the open door, waving for her to hurry. Dobyns pushed off the wall and ran for safety.

A muffled moan from behind made her glance over her shoulder. Gibson burst through the doorway, its left hand missing and its chest and face pocked by shrapnel. Upon seeing its meal, it charged.

Bellemah wrapped his right hand around the handle on the bulkhead to the side of the door and reached out to pull Dobyns to safety.

"Let me know when," said Robson.

"I will."

Dobyns dove, her chest landing hard on the floor of the helicopter, her legs dangling over the side. Bellemah grabbed the private's belt and leaned back.

"Now!"

Robson pulled back on the stick, lifting the Seahawk off the roof and out over the parking lot. Dobyns clutched for something to hold onto while Bellemah held her in place by the belt.

At the end of the roof, Gibson jumped onto the ledge and dove. It grabbed Dobyns' left leg as it fell, ripping the private out of the cabin and yanking Bellemah with them.

Alissa made her way over to the troop door and leaned over the edge. She watched as they fell toward the ground, all three bodies leaving splotches of blood on the white snow when they impacted. Alissa said a silent prayer for them and slid shut the door.

"Is she aboard?" asked Robson.

"No. A deader got her."

"Fuck." Robson sighed then keyed his microphone. "Home Plate, this is Sky King. I've rescued the two civilians and have retrieved the blood samples. All Marines on the retrieval team, my crew chief, and my security element are KIA. Do you copy? Over."

"We copy, Sky King. What are you going to do now? Over."

"I'm heading back to Warren Island per Colonel Williams' request. I think I can make it back before the storm gets too heavy. Over."

"Roger that, Sky King. We'll radio Warren Island and let them know you're coming. Good luck. Over and out."

"What happens now?" asked Alissa.

"Just sit back and relax. We should be home in about an hour and a half."

Alissa sat beside Chris and visually examined his wound. A gash three inches long and an inch deep cut across his leg. Blood flowed down the skin and soaked the lower half of his pants.

"How does it feel?"

"It hurts like hell. All that running didn't help it any."

"It looks like the bleeding has slowed." She leaned closer to the wound. "May I?"

"Be my guest."

Alissa pulled aside the tear in his pants to get a better view. She placed her forefingers on either side of the wound and pulled it apart. Chris tensed and gasped.

"Sorry."

"That's okay."

Alissa examined the gash for a few seconds then removed her hands. "No permanent damage was done. It'll need stitches. We'll fix you up when we get back to Warren Island. But it's going to hurt to walk on it for a few weeks."

"Good." Chris forced a smile. "I could use some bed rest."

Alissa went over to the first aid kit hanging on the bulkhead and removed a roll of gauze. She wrapped it around the wound several times, ignoring Chris' grunts. When finished, she tore the last foot in half and used the two ends to secure the bandage in place. Sitting back in the seat, she leaned her head against Chris' shoulder.

The only sounds inside the cabin were the thumping of the rotor blades, the swooshing of the windshield wipers, and the gusts of wind buffeting the helicopter from the storm. Within a few minutes, Alissa had fallen asleep.

Chapter Twenty

A SUDDEN JARRING shook Alissa out of her slumber. She awoke with a start, expecting deaders. Instead, she remembered her and Chris were aboard the Seahawk heading back to Warren Island. Chris slumped against the corner of the cabin sound asleep. At least he rested.

The helicopter bucked a second time. Alissa grew concerned. She put on her helmet and spoke into the microphone.

"Is everything all right?"

"We're fine," answered Robson. "It's turbulence from the blizzard."

Alissa glanced out the starboard window. It snowed so heavily she could not see the ground. "How high up are we?"

"Five hundred feet. We're experiencing white out conditions."

Concern became anxiety. "Are we in any danger?"

"I'm flying high enough to avoid trees and power lines."

"How will we find the base?"

"Sparks left on a navigational beam. I'm homing in on that. I haven't been able to reach him on the radio. More than likely the storm is interfering."

Alissa wished they had flown back to the *Iwo Jima*. "How long before we get there?"

"We should arrive in a few minutes."

Thank God, Alissa thought. She looked outside one more time, unnerved by not being able to see anything but snow. Turning to Chris, she gently nudged him.

He opened his eyes and smiled. "I must have died and gone to heaven because I see an angel."

Alissa grinned. "We'll be back at base soon."

Chris tilted his head and peered through the windshield. "What's all that?"

"We're in the middle of a blizzard."

"Lovely. We fight off hordes of deaders to crash and burn a few hundred feet from our destination." Chris regretted his comment the moment he saw Alissa tense up. "Sorry. I'm joking."

"I'm not a fan of flying, remember?"

"You can add being an ass to the list of my many faults you keep tabs on."

Alissa squeezed his hand affectionately. "You're good at some things."

The playful banter ended when they heard Robson mumble over the radio, "Shit."

"What's wrong?"

"The lights aren't on at the landing pad. I can't set down there."

"How are we going to land?"

"No problem. The lights are on in the main compound at Islesboro. I'll put it down in the park. It's only a walk of a few hundred feet to the hospital."

Robson turned the helicopter around and headed back to the center of the island. Lights came into view, partly blotted out by the nor'easter. Robson hovered over the compound, choosing the safest spot to land. Slowly he descended, scanning the area beneath him for obstructions. A minute later, the helicopter set down with a jolt.

"Sorry," said Robson. "But as my flight instructor used to say, any landing you can walk away from is a good one. The hospital is across the road to our right."

Alissa squeezed Chris' hand. "Stay here. I'll get a ride."

"I'll go with you. It's not far."

"You always have to play it macho."

Chris winked and pointed his finger at her.

Alissa opened the starboard troop door. A blast of cold air washed through the cabin, bringing with it a swirl of snow. She turned to Chris. "Are you sure you want to do this?"

"I'd rather you carry me."

"Yeah, but no." Alissa removed her helmet and jumped out onto the playground. Five inches of snow already covered the ground. She helped Chris down from the helicopter and, wrapping his left arm over her shoulder, helped him limp toward the hospital.

STATIC CAME THROUGH Robson's helmet with a weak voice trying to break through the background noise. He recognized it as Sparks. "Sky King. Do not…. Repeat… danger… at once."

Robson shut down the engines. As the blades slowed to a stop, he spoke into his microphone. "Sparks, I didn't catch all that. Please repeat."

Sparks did. This time, the message came through clear. Robson ripped the helmet off his head and raced to the cabin, leaning out the open door. Alissa and Chris were a hundred feet from the helicopter.

"Get back here now!"

"What?"

"Get back to the helicopter. The base has been overrun by deaders."

Alissa did not hear him clearly through all the noise, but she didn't need to. The snarling coming from inside the blizzard and the shadows of figures racing toward them through the snow let her know they were about to be swarmed by the living dead.

114

PREVIEW OF
NURSE ALISSA VS. THE ZOMBIES VI: RESCUE

Sorry, there will be no preview of the next book. To do that would be to give away the cliff hanger ending. Consider this book the season finale. Like when JR was shot. Or when Negan bashes one of Rick's people in the head and taunts, "Taking it like a champ." Or when Captain Picard/Locutus of Borg warns the *Enterprise* that resistance was futile and Commander Ryker responds by telling Worf to fire on the Borg ship. All I'll offer is this.

TO BE CONTINUED...

A Thank You to My Readers

I like to think of myself as a storyteller. I've been writing short stories as far back as I can remember, but it was Darren McGavin as *The Night Stalker*'s Carl Kolchak that inspired me to be become a full-time writer. Writing and working for the CIA have been two of the most fulfilling things I've done with my life. The best part is having people who read my books, enjoy them, and want more. I'm extremely fortunate and grateful that I have a fanbase that devours my novels like zombies eating human flesh. You keep reading and I'll keep writing.

If you liked *Nurse Alissa vs. the Zombies V: Desperate Mission*, please post a review on Amazon and/or Goodreads. It doesn't have to be long—just a rating and a sentence or two about why you enjoyed it. The more reviews the *Nurse Alissa vs. the Zombies* series receives, the more opportunity other readers have of discovering the book.

The *Nurse Alissa* saga will continue. Book six is being written and plotted now. Alissa and her group will be teaming up with the military for a bit, which means plenty of deader action and some highly unique ways to kill off the living dead. After that, the (few?) survivors might go on a road trip. New Mexico sounds fun.

A second series, which is more along the lines of paranormal horror, is currently in the works (the other post-apocalypse series has been postponed indefinitely). Expect the first book in that series sometime in early 2021.

Acknowledgments

Writing is done in a vacuum. Getting published, on the other hand, is a complicated process involving many people, all of whom deserve to be recognized.

Once again, I want to thank my Beta readers, the unsung heroes of writers. No matter how many times you edit and proofread your manuscript, errors always make it through. My Beta readers, especially Dan Uebel and Doc Fried, provide detailed notes on the spelling/grammatical/punctuation mistakes I missed and help me not to look illiterate.

A major debt of thanks goes to J.R. Jackson, a former U.S. Navy Chief Petty Officer and author of the *Up From the Depths* series. There is a heavy military element in this book and, being a civilian, I reached out for assistance. Thank God. J.R. read the manuscript and provided numerous suggestions on how to bring the book in line with military policies and procedures. This book would have read a lot less realistic if not for J.R. However, certain protocols I had to abandon for the sake of the plot, so any scenes that don't pass the guffaw factor are my responsibility.

Christian Bentulan designed the cover art for *Nurse Alissa vs. the Zombies V: Desperate Mission* as well as the other books in the saga. I love Christian's work. His covers reach out and grab the reader's attention as well as foreshadow what is to come. Plus, Archer appears on each cover, which he appreciates. (Truthfully, he doesn't. Like his namesake in the series, the real Archer is also an asshat. But my fans love to see him on the cover.)

You would not be reading this book, or any of the other in

the *Nurse Alissa* series, were it not for my dear friend and colleague Alina Giuchici. I hadn't written a zombie series since *Rotter Apocalypse* was published in 2015. Alina is a major fan of my stories and kept urging me to go back to writing about the living dead. With some gentle shoving in the right direction and a few well-placed ideas, over the course of a long week on the road I came up with the concept of the Alissa series. If you like these books, be sure to thank Alina.

Finally, a major debt of thanks goes to my family, human and furry. This is the first book I've written since returning to being a full-time writer. Rather than seeing this as an opportunity for more free time, like so many writers, I see this as my chance to get more written. In my old job I used to start work at 0400; now that's often the time I go to bed (I'm a night owl by nature). I couldn't do this without their love and support.

About the Author

Scott M. Baker was born and raised in Everett, Massachusetts and spent twenty-three years in northern Virginia working for the Central Intelligence Agency. Scott is now retired and lives just outside of Concord, New Hampshire with his wife and fellow writer Alison Beightol, stepdaughter, two rambunctious boxers, and two cats who treat him as their human servant. He is currently writing the *Nurse Alissa vs. the Zombies* saga, his latest zombie apocalypse series. Previous works include the *Shattered World* series, his five-book young adult post-apocalypse thriller about a group of adventurers attempting to close interdimensional portals into Hell; *The Vampire Hunters* trilogy, about humans fighting the undead in Washington D.C.; *Rotter World, Rotter Nation,* and *Rotter Apocalypse,* his first post-apocalyptic zombie saga; *Yeitso,* his homage to the giant monster movies of the 1950s that he loved watching as a kid; as well as several zombie-themed novellas and anthologies.

Please check out Scott's social media accounts for the latest information on future books, upcoming events, and other fun stuff.

Blog: scottmbakerauthor.blogspot.com
Facebook: facebook.com/groups/397749347486177
Twitter: twitter.com/vampire_hunters
Instagram: instagram.com/scottmbakerwriter

www.ingramcontent.com/pod-product-compliance
Lightning Source LLC
Chambersburg PA
CBHW071928220626
47052CB00002B/504